Of Song and Wonder

Tales of Elaris

Robyn Sarty

Of Song and Wonder

TALES OF ELARIS

Robyn Sarty

BELWOOD PUBLISHING

Book Cover by MoorBooks

Edited by Nicole Schroeder

Map by Robyn Sarty

Ebook: 978-1-990223-26-6

Paperback: 978-1-990223-29-7

For Sarah,
who refused to give up on Peadar and Cäcilia.

Glossary

A uthor Note: This story combines Rapunzel with Peter Pan in a fantastical setting that draws loosely from Scottish lore. It is not a Scottish folklore retelling. That said, here are some of the unusual terms and definitions that fit this story, along with the pronunciation of some of the character names:

Aerlisse (Arr-lees) — A bird with bright blue feathers

Cù dhearg (Que Derg) — A red dog, often used as a messenger between the realm of humans and the realm of faeries

Daoine Sith (Doon-ya Shee) — The term faeries use when referring to themselves

Faery — A race of beings that look like humans but are often shorter in stature; they have wings they can hide and magical abilities.

Glaistig (Glass-chick) — The faery term for witch

Tìr nan Òg — The realm of faeries

Characters:

Peadar (Pah-der)

Cäcilia (Tse-tsi-lia)

Amaran (Ah-mar-an)

Branwen (Brahn-wen)

Eoinan (Oh-in-an)

Jowan (Joh-an)

Maelore (May-lor)

Mara (Mah-rah)

Thalion (Thal-yun)

Places:

An Dorchadas (Un Dor-kha-dus) — The island where prisoners are exiled

Baileglas (Bally-glass) — Capital of Tìr nan Òg

Castil (Cas-til) — Capital of the Torician Empire

Elpida (El-pee-da) — Human country at war with Toricia

Never Isles — Hidden islands that are part of Tìr nan Òg, encompassing the island Peadar lives on as well as An Dorchadas

Tìr nan Òg — Land of the faeries; it has a vague geographical location, but it mostly exists in another dimension.

Torician Empire (Tor-i-she-an) — Largest of the human nations

Elpída
Dunkeld
Principality of Drotthem
Tír'nan Óg
Torician Empire
Sotiello
Zielmeil

Prologue

The flash of magic that rippled across the sky sent Cäcilia scrambling to the window. Shimmers of color flared in all directions, creating a cascade of light.

She fell to her knees in wonder, leaning against the windowsill. She wiped tears from her cheeks, careful not to blur her vision. The rainbow that filled the sky was the most beautiful thing she had ever seen, and she wanted to hold onto the memory forever, to sear it into the inside of her eyelids so it would be the last thing she ever saw.

Standing carefully, not taking her eyes off the sky, she leaned out the window. The ground far below her tower hosted a garden of lavender, posies, and more, but the dainty flowers were nothing compared with the riot of color overhead.

As the rainbow paled to the familiar azure blue, Cäcilia slid to the floor with her eyes closed, desperate to hold onto the image. Her vision might've been slowly fading, but at least she had the memory of the colors chasing each other across the sky to hold onto when she could see no more.

Chapter One

T he view out the tower window was one of delight and
    wonder, though Cäcilia saw none of it. With her eyes
closed, she swayed in time with the music pouring from her
violin, but even opening them wouldn't have made a difference.
Over the past months, her vision had deteriorated to the point
she could no longer see the difference between the greens of the
forest-covered hills or the rich blue of the river.

The sun pouring in her window provided enough light for
her to see shapes, though the meager furnishings of the tower room hadn't moved in the eighteen years she'd lived there.
Knowing precisely where everything was kept her from banging
into them — and her hair from tangling around them.

She turned her face to the warm rays, imaging the sap-
phire-blue feathers of the aerlisse soaking up the sun as the
birds danced across the sky. Her earliest memories were filled
with the dazzling sight, but only recently had she thought to

capture them in song. The endeavor was proving harder than she expected.

If only the birds would fly close to her tower again, that she might hear their song and feel their flight on the wind. The last time she remembered hearing them was the day Amaran had left. Even before that, they had been coming less frequently.

Cäcilia blamed the couple who had visited the castle months before.

Ever since then, the world had felt different. Amaran was gone more. The birds sang less. The colors had been less vibrant.

She couldn't really blame the last one on them though. They weren't the cause of the blindness that had been progressing since she was a child.

She missed colors the most.

When she thought about the couple, she saw silver and gold, wrapped in soft purple.

Amaran was black with a blue that rivaled the aerlisse's feathers.

Right, the aerlisse. She brought her thoughts back to the song she was composing about the birds. She adjusted the soft cloth for her chin and raised the bow to the strings again. The first few bars were perfect — gentle, lilting notes that rose to the trilling song of an early morning. Then came the measures that reminded her of their rich color and poise, and she smiled as she played the notes where they stretched forth their wings to launch into flight.

And then nothing.

Her fingers stilled on the strings as she tried to imagine the correct notes to capture the playful elegance of the aerlisse on the wind.

She tried an arpeggio and frowned, then a variation. No, neither would do. Her fingers found the handful of notes that sounded right, and she played around with them, straining to find the next step. Maybe if she started down a third and ran up... No, that wasn't right either. She went back to the last section that was correct and played again, playing it faster than she normally would in the hopes that her fingers would find something new if she raced toward the edge. She reached the last note, and there was nothing but empty air and a yearning for flight.

She dropped the bow to her side in frustration. The last time the aerlisse had flown by her tower was too long ago. She couldn't remember enough to capture them. Shuffling forward, she felt for the end of the bed with her foot. With the bow and violin in one hand, she ran her other over the quilt until she found the corner of the case. The violin nestled into its spot with ease, and she laid the soft chin cloth over it. A twist of the screw at the end of the bow released the tension on the horsehair before she placed it carefully on the hook on the lid of the case.

She lowered the lid of the wooden box, ensuring nothing was caught on the edge before fastening the buckles. She picked it up by the handle on the lid and moved to the wall, where she lowered the case into its assigned spot.

Straightening with a groan, she stretched her back, then lifted her hair to give her neck muscles a break. She hummed as she moved to the other side of the tower. Even with her eyes still closed, she stepped with confidence.

Well, as much confidence as one could have while also having to push swathes of hair out of the way. Amaran had never given a clear explanation for why Cäcilia's hair grew to such lengths, but she always seemed perturbed when the girl asked about it.

Her toe bumped softly against the cupboard that stood against the wall, and with deft hands, she found the cup and pitcher and poured herself some water.

A trilling call outside the window sent her heart racing. Were the aerlisse back? She spun around, setting the pitcher down as she moved.

The pitcher landed on the edge, tumbling to the floor. Water splashed over her feet, quickly absorbed by the hair that pooled there.

"No, no, no," she murmured, crouching down to find the water jug. She lifted it slowly in an effort to preserve the last of the water, but no pleasing slosh met her ears as she tipped the pitcher.

Without Amaran, she had no way of getting more water.

Cäcilia sank to the floor, tears filling her eyes. Was this to be her life? Trapped in darkness, unable to see beyond her tower, alone?

"Amaran? Where are you?" she whispered.

Chapter Two

Peadar balanced on the topmost branch of the tallest tree on his island, his wings fluttering just enough to battle the wind that had driven away the clouds.

The neighboring island had been hidden behind a heavy bank of fog for as long as he could remember. But something had changed a few months ago, and now not only could An Dorchadas be seen from the Never Isles, but he had also discovered that Tìr nan Òg was much closer than he'd realized.

Peadar watched the prisoners across the water navigate the island on foot with a slight shudder. Being exiled was one thing, but for a faery to have a collar of iron limiting their magic, their ability to fly... That was an altogether crueler punishment.

The newest inhabitant of the island had no wings with which to take flight, however. And while the faeries accepted their fate, this fellow had made several attempts to escape. What the fool didn't realize was that there was no way from An Dorchadas back to Tìr nan Òg.

Peadar stepped off the branch and fell, letting his wings catch the wind. With a few quick beats, he rose above the trees again and headed for the mainland, a grin spreading across his face. With the fog gone, getting to Tìr nan Òg from the Never Isles was easy. None of the magical barriers around An Dorchadas extended this far.

He noticed the new prisoner watching him, so Peadar flipped onto his back and waved jauntily at the man. Whatever he had done to be exiled was more than enough reason to be teased.

The wind over the open water buffeted him, and Peadar turned into it. A few minutes of skillful flying, and he reached the mainland. With a whoop, he dove down into the trees, twisting and turning among their branches. Every tree on the Never Isles was mapped on his mind, so he could fly through them with his eyes closed. But the unfamiliar forest offered a challenge he'd been yearning for.

He struck out toward the river he'd found the last time he'd gone adventuring. It supposedly flowed into a huge loch where lived a monster of untold size. He laughed. Wouldn't that be an adventure? To find a monster — maybe to fight it, maybe to friend it!

Peadar's green and brown clothing blended well with the landscape of the Never Isles, but here on Tìr nan Òg, everything was brighter and bolder. Trees were so green they looked blue. Flowers fairly glowed with pinks and oranges, and even the clouds that dotted the sky were alive with color.

Diving low, he skimmed over the river, trailing his hand through the water. A song filled his senses, and he danced in time to the notes. His eyes drifted to a close, and he soared upward as the music commanded, pirouetting and twirling.

Abruptly the song ended, and his wings stopped beating in time. He tumbled through the air toward the river, catching himself with his nose a hair's breadth from the frigid water.

"Get it together, Peadar," he scolded himself as he rose on steady wings once again. "You had a bath once this year already. No need for a second, especially not in that."

He carried on, watching for the monster from the loch, but the distant song teased him as snippets reached him. At last, when the music was the loudest, he turned away from the river.

To his disgust, the music seemed to have died away. But he was curious now, and he made it his goal to always satisfy his curiosity if he could.

Something peculiar stood out among the blue-green trees, and at once he knew that must be where the song came from. He flitted downward, circling the crumbling stone structure that hid among the forest.

Only one tower of the old castle still stood proudly, the rest left to disrepair. A single window faced the river near the top of the tower and drew him closer. With whisper-quiet wings, he flew up to the open portal.

A narrow bed was tucked into a near corner, covered in a quilt of flowers that rivaled the glades he had flown through. A table with two chairs and a cupboard sat against the far wall.

And on the floor sat a girl, her face buried in her hands as her shoulders shook with sobs.

He pulled back, not wanting to intrude on her anguish. But the sorrow that wrapped around her brought him back.

"Miss?" he said softly.

A desperate need to help filled him. He climbed through the window, his feet tangling in a strange material that carpeted the floor. Not wanting to fight with it, he rose in the air and flew to her side.

"Miss? Are you all right?"

The young woman screamed, flailing as she tried to stand. She held a pitcher in her hand — a pitcher that connected with his jaw and sent him spiraling backward.

"Oy!" he protested, clutching his face. He paused among the rafters to catch his breath.

"Who's there?" she demanded, pressing her back into the corner of the cupboard and the wall. She wielded the pitcher like a weapon.

"It's me," Peadar said, floating to a stop in front of her.

She tilted her face upward, eyes searching the rafters he'd just vacated. "Who's 'me'?"

He cocked his head, curious about the way she seemed to look right past him, as though his shadow, dancing on the wall behind him, held more substance than he did. "Huh," he said as he drifted to a stand. His feet immediately tangled in the strange, silky fibers.

"Ouch!" she cried, her free hand clutching her head.

He looked down at the fibers wrapped around his feet, then back at her.

Hair. He was standing in piles of hair.

Chapter Three

There was a strange man in her tower, and he was standing on her hair.

Cäcilia brandished the water pitcher in the direction of the shadowy shape, hoping it would be enough to ward him off. Not that a blind girl waving around a metal jug was likely to frighten anyone.

"I'm not going to hurt you," he said in a soft, lilting accent, not unlike Amaran's.

"Then why are you here?"

"You were crying."

His voice was coming to the right of the shadow, and she shifted her gaze that direction. A form appeared in the dim light.

Oh. She'd been focused on his shadow against the white-washed wall.

She squinted, trying to make out his features, but with her growing headache and tear-blurred vision, he was nothing more than a shape. The tower room was gloomier than she had expected. Had she lost track of time playing? It wouldn't have been the first time.

"You're standing on my hair," she said at last.

He immediately shifted, and the ache in her neck eased. "Sorry! I'm so sorry!" he exclaimed, his voice coming from higher than before. But that was silly. There was nothing for him to stand on.

"Thank you," she said, her voice prim. She turned, her hand searching for the corner of the cupboard. Carefully, she searched the worktop until she found the teapot centered at the back, then set the water pitcher two fingerbreadths to the left. She took her time adjusting the handle before turning back to the man.

Maybe he'd be gone by the time she did, as quickly as he'd appeared.

One could hope.

"Is there anything I can do for you?" he asked.

So much for wishes coming true.

"Thank you, no. I am quite well." How tall was he? His voice still sounded like it was coming from far above her head.

"You were crying. By yourself. In a tower." A rumble of thunder punctuated his words.

"You needn't keep pointing that out."

"I'm sorry — I just would like to help, if I can?"

Help. What did she need help with? A thought suddenly struck her.

"How did you get in?"

"Through the window."

"Ah." So much for that idea. She couldn't follow him out to fetch more water.

"How do you get in and out?" he asked in return.

The light was almost completely gone now, but she resisted the urge to close her eyes. Letting this stranger know she couldn't see wasn't wise.

"I don't."

"You...don't? You don't leave the tower? Ever?"

"No. It's not safe for me out there." But Amaran had been gone so long...

Another rumble of thunder shook the tower, and she cringed. Spinning back to the cupboard, she grabbed the water pitcher and hurried to the narrow table. She set the pitcher in place just as the sky opened and rain poured through a hole in the thatched roof.

Wind howled around the tower, driving rain in through the narrow window.

"It's not safe for you in here!" he pointed out. "We should go find somewhere better to stay." His voice raised to be heard over the storm.

"This is safe!" she argued. Who was this stranger to tell her that her home was unsafe?

She clutched the water pitcher, feeling the *plink* of every drop that fell from the ceiling as the storm continued outside. She didn't want him to be right. A pile of thatch collapsed on her bed.

She sighed. The tower had never been a cozy place to wait out a storm. Ever since she was a child, she had hated it. Would Amaran really expect her to stay here in a leaky tower?

"Fine. But you're going to have to help braid my hair first." Braiding her hair would give her time to think. Amaran often went on foraging trips, leaving her alone for days at a time. But never for this long. Her guardian wouldn't abandon her like that, and the sense that something was wrong wrapped around her again.

She separated her hair into the usual nine pieces and began working, her fingers deftly weaving through the long strands as she showed him what to do.

She wasn't prepared for how intimate it would feel to have his hands running through her scalp, brushing against her neck, sending shivers across her skin. Or maybe that was the rain being blown against her from the hole in the roof.

"Is this right?" he asked.

She adjusted her grip on her braid to hold it in one hand and reached the other up to her head to feel for the braid. Her fingers brushed his, and she jerked away. Then his hand wrapped around hers, warmth seeping into her fingers as he guided her to feel where he'd been working.

She swallowed hard, trying to focus on the braid. It wasn't as even as she would have done, but she wasn't about to complain. "That's good," she said, her voice sounding strange.

At last all her hair was braided together. "You said you came in through the window. I'm assuming you have a way to get back down?"

"Nope." He sounded far too smug.

"Explain."

"Do you trust me?"

"Frankly, no. We just met, and the only reason I'm going with you is to find out what happened to my guardian."

He laughed, and she had to admit that she appreciated he was so vocal about his reactions. So often she struggled to understand Amaran, with her reserved mannerisms and tendency to speak with her facial expressions.

"Fair enough," the man said. "But you're going to need to for this. Do you have everything?"

"My violin!" She hurried over to the wall and picked it up by the handle.

He placed a hand on the violin. "You can't carry that in this storm. Here, let's put it under the bed to protect it."

She hesitated, feeling the weight of his hands on the case. She hated to leave it behind, but the violin was more likely to be damaged if she brought it with her. The case was heavy, and she wouldn't be able to carry it for long.

"Wrap it in the quilt, please," she said as she relinquished it, rubbing her eyes with her other hand.

He did so with quick movements, then dropped the other blanket over her head. "I'm guessing, as you've never been outside, that you don't have a cloak, so this will have to do."

She opened her mouth to protest as a memory of running through the grass flashed through her mind, but that was ridiculous. To cover her awkwardness, she moved to the small door set into the wall and tugged it open. Amaran had said the items inside were hers, but she mustn't ever touch them. But the brooch seemed like the best option to hold the blanket in place, so she scrambled among the items until the cool metal met her fingers. The gold filigree encased a large stone of a rich plum color that she'd never forgotten, no matter how long ago she'd looked at it.

With a bit of help from the man, she pinned the blanket in place and turned to face him, just barely able to discern his shape through the gloom. "What now?"

She heard his grin through his words as he held out his hands to her. "Trust me."

Swallowing back her concerns, she placed her hand in his. Her feet lifted off the floor, and she grabbed at him with her other hand.

He laughed, a sound that clashed with the storm overhead, yet somehow it allayed her fears. He tugged her hand and she followed, trusting that this stranger, a man whose name she didn't even know, would keep her safe.

"Trust me," he said again, this time just above a whisper.

She nodded, her own voice refusing to work. "I do."

He guided her out the window, and she was immediately tossed around by the wind, the weight of her hair pulling her down. Strong hands grabbed her arm, and he shouted over the storm.

"I promise not to let go."

Chapter Four

A core advantage to being queen of Tìr nan Òg lay in being able to place portals to the human realm wherever she wished.

Which was especially beneficial today because if she had to spend any more time among the Torician Senate than necessary, she was going to break something.

Primarily the smarmy face of the so-called president.

Mara strode through the marble halls with no regard for the soldiers who would arrest her in an instant if they saw her. She fed a little more magic into the illusion that surrounded her to ensure she remained hidden. The urge to splash a bit of color over the monochromatic walls tugged at her, but she held back her magic, her anger stronger than the desire to be petty.

Elpida has had long enough to own up to their crimes. If they continue to insist they don't have the child, we'll raze them to the ground.

How dare he?

After everything she'd done to keep the humans from going to war, they still thirsted after blood. She cast the massive doors open before her and swept past the oblivious guards into the gardens that encircled the senate. Her nose curled at the stench pouring off the humans wrapped in those ridiculous uniforms, which were too heavy for the climate.

Maybe she shouldn't try so hard to hide her presence. Even when she purposefully left clues, the Toricians placed the blame at the feet of their enemies, little thinking she was the bigger threat.

She would have to return Cäcilia.

Until she did, the Toricians would continue to blame their neighbor to the north, Elpida, for kidnapping the child. The fools.

When she'd taken the child, she had left a message: Stop the aggression, and the baby will be returned unharmed.

Instead, the threats had broken into an all-out war, and despite repeated messages, the Toricians ignored her, convinced Elpida had stolen the baby.

The northern nation was flagging from the continued onslaught, and Toricia had decided one last concentrated battle would destroy their enemies for good. A week of listening in on their senate meetings and doing her best to manipulate the council had done nothing to assuage them.

Never mind that all their spies had failed to find any sign of the child on the peninsula. With the girl's paler skin and gray eyes, she would stand out among the Elpidans.

The rowan tree was unique among the other plants as the only tree to bear fruit and flowers year round, but the bumbling Toricians hadn't managed to kill it, despite their best efforts. She laid her hand against the trunk, steeling herself for the sudden weightlessness as the world swirled around her.

She shut her eyes against the mesmerizing colors and opened them just as the portal opened above her castle.

Annoyed to find that rain was falling instead of the clear crisp air she'd been longing for, she flew straight for the tower, careful to circle around the back to stay out of sight of the window.

Mud squelched under her feet as she walked around the tower, leaning close to the chilled stones for some shelter from the rain.

"Cäcilia! Let down your hair!" she called.

Only silence greeted her. Tilting her head back, she peered through the rain for signs of movement. But the window remained dark and still. The forgetful child hadn't even bothered to light a lamp.

Mara felt a twinge of guilt. Time passed faster in Tìr nan Òg than in the human realm, so Cäcilia had been alone longer than she'd intended.

"Cäcilia! I'm back!" she called again.

Annoyed, and slightly worried, she shook out her wings and launched herself into the falling rain. "If she's fallen asleep..." she muttered under her breath. Hiding Cäcilia here had meant hiding the fact she was in faery land — and therefore the fact that Mara was a faery. She had never let the girl see that she could fly.

"Cäcilia!" If the girl responded now, she'd do her best to hide — which wouldn't be hard with the girl's failing vision.

The window remained empty, even as she climbed through it. Water poured from a hole in the roof, covering the floor. In a panic, she flew across the small room, even allowing her magic to light the space. Cäcilia wasn't curled in her bed, or seated at the table, or working at the bench.

She was gone.

Chapter Five

Peadar led Cäcilia through the rain-drenched trees. The water was making it hard to keep her hand tightly in his, and with the looming darkness, he wanted to find someplace to rest for the night soon. Perhaps it would have been wiser to stay in the tower with some shelter, but he hated being confined, and she'd looked so lost — he had to do something.

It had been a while since Peadar had flown with a human, but it never ceased to amaze him how the magic extended from him into their bodies. He had to concentrate on flying, on moving his wings, but as long as Cäcilia held tight, she stayed aloft with him.

The rain began to lift, making their flight through the trees easier. He forced himself to go slower than he otherwise would, knowing he wouldn't be able to weave through the trees with her beside him. He glanced over to see if she was okay. His heart lifted at the look of wonder on her face. Her free hand was stretched out, brushing against the dripping leaves. Her head was thrown back, her mouth open to catch the falling rain.

"Do you like it?" he asked.

She laughed, and the trees danced in response to the sound. "It's magic!"

"It is!" But something in her tone made him think she didn't realize how true that was.

A blue glow ahead drew him forward, and he guided her into a circle of trees where the rain didn't fall and the flowers shone with the light of the moon. A peace settled over them, cocooning them from the outside world.

He glided to a stop, ensuring her feet settled on a smooth patch of moss before letting her hand slip from his. Cäcilia turned in a slow circle, squinting at the colors. She gathered her hair up to keep from tripping on it.

"What is this place?" she asked.

"A faery glen," he told her.

"Faery? Is that what you are?" She didn't turn to look at him.

He frowned, wondering if there was something wrong with her eyes. He shook his head at himself. That was a silly question. Of course there was something wrong — look at how she acted.

"Are you all right?" he asked.

"Of course," she replied, though he wasn't sure he believed her.

"So you are a faery, then?" she said softly. "I've never met a faery before."

How did she live in that tower if she hadn't seen a faery? There were no doors, no stairs. Only a faery could access the window like he had.

"I am."

"And...you have wings?" she tilted her head, looking at him.

He nodded, then remembered to say aloud, "Yes."

If he was questioning her eyesight, she wouldn't be able to see his nodding.

"How come I can't see them?" she asked.

He laughed. "I can hide them." He concentrated on making them glow more.

"Oh, I think I can see them now," she said with a small laugh.

He moved the iridescent green wings softly, slowly.

"Oh!" she exclaimed in wonder, then rubbed her eyes, which looked even more red now.

"Here." He took her hand and guided her to a seat nestled in the roots of a tree. "Stay here, and I'll be right back."

"Where are you going?" she asked, letting her head rest against the tree with her eyes closed.

"Not far," he promised. "Tell me about your tower." He flitted across the glen to a bush covered in shimmering pink berries and started gathering them in his hand.

"It's a tower." She shrugged, then let her hand fall to the moss beside her, running it over the spongy growth until she found one of the flowers. Her delicate fingers played over the stalks, caressing the petals with a feather-light touch.

"But it's in the middle of Tìr nan Òg, yet you've never seen a faery? How is that possible?" he asked. The berries tumbled from his hand, so he lifted the tail of his tunic to form a small hammock and filled it with more berries.

"I guess because I've never left my tower," she said quietly.

"You've never left your tower? Really? Your entire life, you stayed within the tower?" he asked incredulously as he returned to her side with the berries and two rocks.

"Yes," she said a little defensively.

"How come?" he asked, but he wasn't sure he wanted to know the answer. There were ways that faeries could draw power from humans in Tìr nan Òg, as vile as that may be.

And a human girl trapped in a tower would be a captive source of power. He smashed the berries between the two rocks with more force than necessary. Cäcilia jolted at the sound. "What are you doing?"

"Making a paste for your eyes," he replied, finishing grinding the berries between the stones.

"My eyes?"

"Yes, to help soothe them."

She hugged her knees to her chest, thinking a moment before she replied. "I'm going blind. No paste is going to heal that."

"Maybe not," he said, "but your eyes look sore and red. This will at least help them feel better. May I?"

She nodded, and he leaned forward, carefully smearing the bright pink paste on his fingers. She flinched as his knuckle brushed her cheek.

"I'm sorry," he whispered, pausing his movements.

"No, it's all right," she replied softly. "It's just...been a while since anyone has touched me."

"I held your hand earlier," he teased.

She laughed gently. "But that was a necessity."

"Maybe not," he murmured. "May I continue?"

She nodded her permission, and he drew closer, his careful fingers brushing the paste against her eyelids.

"Please...what is it?" she asked, her breath fluttering against his wrist.

"Faery berries," he replied. "They have some healing properties. The paste won't fix everything immediately, but it should help."

She nodded again. "Where do you think Amaran went?" she asked, changing the subject.

Peadar gave a small shrug. "That's hard to say. Where does she normally go?"

"She doesn't tell me. She doesn't tell me many things," Cäcilia admitted.

"And she leaves you alone in the tower with no food or resources?"

"She's never been gone this long before. I spend my time playing the violin and studying — at least, I did before my vision got too bad — so the time always flies by."

Peadar pressed his lips together to hide his anger. He didn't know who this Amaran was, but despite Cäcilia's innocent testimony, he doubted the woman's intentions were pure. Who kept a girl locked in a tower with no way to escape?

"How long were you in the tower?" he asked.

"My whole life — eighteen years."

Peadar struggled to hide his shock. "Eighteen years...and you've never been outside?"

"Amaran said it wasn't safe."

She had a small red mark on her jaw. It interrupted the perfection of her face, yet made her all the more alluring. "And you never wanted to leave?"

"Oh, yes, all the time when I was a child, but Amaran always said there were too many dangers and that it was better to stay indoors. She said anything I needed to see in the world was right outside my window, and for a long time, she was right. I saw so many wonderful things...and then..." She paused. "Then my eyesight started to fade, and I couldn't see as much anymore. But sometimes...I wonder if there were fewer things to see, and not my eyes failing me."

Peadar nodded. Even in the Never Isles, he had sensed changes. The magic had shifted over the years.

"In recent years, yes," he said. "Magic — it's what causes the colors, the birds, the wonders."

"I just thought maybe my memories of the rainbow clouds and the flowers were just childhood imagination."

"No." He shook his head. "Something's happened to the magic."

"A few months ago, there was a light," Cäcilia recalled. "It was beautiful, but things felt different after that. Of course, now I can't see enough to know if the colors have all returned."

Peadar thought back. A few months ago was when the fog had lifted around Tír nan Óg, when he first started venturing back to the mainland.

"I don't know what caused that," he admitted. "But you're right — something shifted."

"Do you think Amaran was involved?"

"No. She wouldn't...but..." Cäcilia hesitated, as if remembering something.

"Are you sure she's not a faery?" Peadar asked quietly.

"She's not...well, I've never seen her fly. I've never seen her with wings."

"But we can hide our wings," he reminded her. "If she didn't fly, how did she escape the tower?"

"I assumed there was a staircase or something," she admitted. "One I couldn't find. When I got older, and my hair grew long enough, we used that to help her climb in and out."

Peadar decided to drop the subject. He didn't want to distress her. "I'm Peadar, by the way."

"Cäcilia," she replied with a slight smile.

"All done!" he proclaimed, leaning back to admire his handiwork. The pink paste shimmered on her eyelids, and he felt a strange urge to kiss them. Clearing his throat, he stood.

"Excuse me. I'll go wash up."

"Is there water? I spilled mine back at the tower before you came," she said.

"Of course," he replied. He took her hand and guided her along the path, berating himself for not remembering the empty water pitcher earlier.

As they walked, the way Cäcilia kept her slender hand in his sent shivers up his arm, filling him with a sense of protectiveness. He had promised her they would find Amaran, but now he wanted to find her for another reason — to confront her for leaving Cäcilia alone for so long.

Chapter Six

The next morning, Cäcilia woke with the dawn. The air was filled with the chirping of birds and hidden creatures. It was noisier than the tower. She opened her eyes and was relieved to find they weren't painful and sore as they had been so often of late. Blinking, she gazed at the beautiful colors around her. Maybe there was magic in the paste after all, for she could see more clearly than she had in a long time. She could make out the shapes of trees, the soft green moss beneath her fingers...or was it blue moss? She would have to ask about that. Across the glen, she spotted a form in green topped with gold that she took to be Peadar.

Her mind wandered to what they had discussed about Amaran. Was Amaran really trustworthy? She didn't want to question her guardian's intentions, but something in how Peadar had reacted to her story had left a hollow feeling. She blinked again, hearing a strange hissing sound nearby.

A few feet away, a tiny creature clung to a branch, its ears almost as big as its head, with a long tail curling around the tree.

"Oh..." she breathed, squinting at it, "it's the cutest thing I've ever seen!" She longed to bury her fingers in its soft white fur. She'd read about animals that had delightfully soft coats.

"Is that...a kitten?" she wondered aloud as she stood up, her blanket falling to the ground. She had never seen one in real life before, but it seemed close to what she had imagined.

She took a hesitant step forward, not wanting to scare it. "Hi, precious," she whispered. "Don't be afraid. Aren't you the sweetest?"

But as she reached out her hand, the creature hissed savagely, baring sharp teeth. She flinched back.

"It's okay," she crooned, reaching out again, her fingers brushing the soft fur.

"Cäcilia, no!" Peadar shouted. In an instant, he grabbed the back of her dress and yanked her away.

She screamed as he pulled her back.

Peadar leaped into the air, dragging her with him. "Look!" he cried.

Cäcilia peered around. The branches were swarming with white blobs — more of the creatures. "I didn't know kittens were like that!" she exclaimed. She pulled her arms in close, but with Peadar holding her by the back of her dress, she had limited movement.

"That's not a kitten!" he shouted. "Quick, give me your hand!"

She reached up, and he pulled her up beside him, relieving the pressure on her dress. "Not kittens — they're fluffkins!" he panted.

One of the creatures leaped from a branch, nearly brushing Peadar's boot. He kicked it away with a sharp cry, sending the fluffkin tumbling to the ground.

"Peadar! What did you do?" she cried in horror.

"Hold on!" he shouted, swooping higher through the sky. "We've got to get away from here!"

It wasn't until they were several minutes away from the glade that Peadar finally slowed down and returned them to the earth.

"Explain yourself," Cäcilia demanded. "What is a fluffkin?"

"A small, deadly creature that likes to lure in its prey."

"They didn't look deadly," she said. "They looked so soft and gentle!"

"Yes, the soft and gentle things that hiss at you and try to bite your face off," Peadar said sarcastically.

"Maybe it was just afraid?"

"There were hundreds of them, Cäcilia. How do you not know about fluffkins?"

"I lived in a tower!" she retorted.

"Right..." He ran a hand through his hair, and she watched the top of his outline grow spiked. "Well, fluffkins are some of the most vicious predators in Tìr nan Óg. They hunt in packs and lure prey with their cuteness. Most creatures know better, but they've been known to swarm and trap much larger prey."

"How much larger?"

"Unicorn-sized," Peadar guessed.

"Unicorns? Now you're just making things up!" She crossed her arms as she glared at him.

"I thought you said you were educated?"

"I was!"

"Then how do you not know anything?"

"I had many books. The history of the continent —"

"The continent?" he interrupted. "Ohhh."

"'Oh,' what?" she demanded.

"You were only taught about human things."

"Excuse me?"

"Amaran hid the fact that she was a faery from you. She didn't tell you about fluffkins, let you believe that unicorns aren't real. Gave you only books about the human realms. She didn't *want* you to know where you were and what else was around."

"Oh." Cäcilia hesitated, letting that sink in, feeling a bit lost. Why wouldn't Amaran have told her the truth?

Chapter Seven

The yellow path curved through the trees ahead of them. Peadar resisted the urge to take to the air. Magic might keep Cäcilia aloft with him, but it was still more tiring for him to fly both of them. And the way she constantly stopped to investigate things that caught her attention told him she would prefer this slower method of travel.

"What's this?" she asked, pointing to a tree with delicate pink flowers and bright red berries. She had taken to checking with him before touching anything lest her curiosity lead her into danger.

"A rowan tree." He pulled a branch down so she could see them up close.

She leaned close, her nose only inches from the little berries. "But it has berries and flowers at the same time. Trees go through cycles of growth. The flowers should all be gone if the berries are this developed."

He grinned at her. "In the human realm, yes. It's a result of winter and the need for trees to be dormant."

"Is there not winter in Tìr nan Òg?"

"You tell me. Do you remember colder temperatures? Snow coating the ground? Flowers dying and trees losing their leaves?"

Her eyes drifted closed as she pondered the question. "No, I guess not." Her eyes reopened and she moved along the path again. "That's interesting — I'd read so much about winter that I took it for granted without properly observing the world around me."

He stepped up beside her. "It's not surprising. In your tower, you were so far above the world that it was hard to observe it."

She slid her arm through his, making his heart skip a beat. "And now that I'm on the ground, I can hardly see them. Will you show me the best things?"

His mouth took a minute to remember how to work. "Of course," he promised. And he meant it. Whatever she asked, whatever she wanted to try, he would find a way to make it happen.

And he knew just where to start. "Come on," he said, upping their pace. "There's a place you'll want to see."

"Where is it?" she said.

"My home," he said simply. But Never Isle was so much more than home. If Tìr nan Òg was a wonder to humans, then Never Isle held the curiosities faeries marveled at.

"What about Amaran?" she asked.

"It would take us years to search all of Tìr nan Òg for her alone. But the Lost Boys will help spread the word."

A soft smile tugged the gentle curve of her cheek. "You would do that for me?"

"Of course. Besides, Never Isle is safer — no vicious fluffkins or giant unicorns." He opted not to tell her about the prisoners on the nearby island. With the barrier, there was no chance of them crossing between the islands. He turned his arm so his palm was facing up. "It's faster if we fly. Are you up for it?"

She slid her hand down his arm to intertwine her fingers with his. "I would love to see your home."

Shaking his wings out, he stepped into the air, and they left the ground behind them. As always, Peadar thrilled with the wonder of soaring through the sky. His wings, all gossamer and shimmer, were nonetheless powerful and responded to his commands to carry them higher with ease.

Cäcilia stared at the world below them. "What are all the colors, please?" She waved her hand before them.

He squinted, trying to see the landscape as she did. "Trees."

"But there's pink ones. And is that purple?" She pointed to a clump some distance ahead.

"Purple and blue and green and yellow," he proclaimed, flying lower so she could see. They flitted from grove to grove, and she collected a leaf from each one.

He landed on a sturdy branch of a tree with metallic blue leaves and pulled another limb close. Cäcilia held the leaves to her nose, studying each one with care before plucking her favorite and tucking it in her pocket with the others.

"If there are so many colors of trees, why did they all look green from my tower?" she asked when they were in the air once more.

Peadar thought about it. "Maybe the ones near your tower tended toward green, so they looked more uniform," he offered. "Although I remember seeing some that should have been yellow..."

He trailed off, a thought niggling at him.

"Really? I wonder why they weren't." She let her fingers trail through the small pink leaves that trembled in their wake.

"Does Amaran have illusion magic?" he asked.

"Illusion magic?"

"Yes, can she make things appear other than what they are?" His own magic tingled at the tips of his fingers.

"I don't know," she said with a sigh. "I didn't even know she was a faery, so I wouldn't have known if she were doing magic."

They flew on, the wind dancing past them. Peadar detoured any time Cäcilia wished to see something up close. At last they reached the shore. A series of gray-green mounds stood against the sharp blue of the sea.

"Which one is Never Isle?" Cäcilia asked. "How long until we get there?"

He grinned at her. "Second to the right, and straight on till morning."

"That long?" she gaped at him.

"No, I'm teasing. It won't take long at all."

He held her hand tightly as they soared over the dazzling waters. He couldn't wait to show her the wonders of Never Isle. Introduce her to the Lost Boys. Keep her safe until they found Amaran.

A plume of brown smoke rose from the center of the island, where the Great Tree stood. The joy trickled out of him like a trail of sparkling dust in his wake. They flew on, ignoring the shore and the cliff he had planned on showing her. She sensed his mood and stayed silent at his side.

"Boys, I'm home!" he called as they landed on the low branch that extended over the glade.

"About time," a languid voice replied.

A human stepped out from the shadows, a sneer marring his face. Peadar shoved Cäcilia behind him as fear rippled through him.

The prisoners had breached the barrier.

Chapter Eight

An uneasy feeling settled over the island. Cäcilia wasn't sure what had happened. Peadar had been furious and had one of the other faeries lead her to a safe place. When he'd joined her later, the anger still rolled off him, but for now he had it contained.

"Will you show me around?" she asked. The sounds carried by the wind excited her imagination, and she wanted to experience everything up close. That, and she wanted to familiarize herself with the area, so she could move about on her own.

"I'm not sure it's safe yet — I have the Lost Boys searching the island for more invaders, but for now, I think we should stay here."

"We could start here. It's so dim that I can't see anything." She'd tried to find her bearings after being left alone, but the dirt floor was covered in roots and stones, and she'd fallen twice before giving up.

Peadar looked down, as if noticing her for the first time. "Why are you on the ground?"

Her cheeks flushed. "I wanted to stay out of the way," she replied primly.

"You fell, didn't you? I'm so sorry." His voice was filled with remorse as he reached down to help her stand.

She flinched at the sudden touch on her arm, then let him help her up. He waved his hand toward the ceiling, and the room filled with a soft glow, enabling her to see more of her surroundings. She let her eyes focus on each thing, allowing them to take shape. The rough table and mismatched chairs filled most of the space, and the far wall held an assortment of cupboards and shelves, all painted different colors. Her gaze continued upward to the arching ceiling, supported by giant twisting roots.

"Oh!" she cried in delight. "We're inside a tree."

"The biggest tree on the island," Peadar said proudly. "This is just our bunker. Normally, we live above."

"Am I...a prisoner?" she asked, turning to him. If this wasn't where they normally lived, why had she been brought down here?

"No!" he cried. "With the intruders, we thought it safer for you to be here. Besides, it's got all the comforts of home — cozy chairs, lots of food..."

She stepped closer to the cupboards, sliding her foot slowly over the ground so she wouldn't trip. She picked up one of the jars, shaking it to confirm her suspicions that it was as empty as the others she could see. "Doesn't seem like a lot of food to me," she teased.

"What? Oh...here." He waved his hand again, and the jar in her hands suddenly weighed much more, and she nearly dropped it.

"Did you just make nuts appear out of nowhere?" she asked in wonder. She dug her hand in and pulled out a few.

He shrugged, beside her now. "Yes and no. They're not real."

Squinting, she rubbed her hand over the bumpy surface of the almond. "It feels real!"

He took it from her. "In all but taste. They vanish when you try to eat them." He tossed it in the air, tilting his head back to catch it. Just before his mouth snapped shut around it, it vanished. She lifted another to her own lips, nipping her finger as the almond ceased to exist when she bit down.

"How is that useful then?" she asked, setting the jar down. All the jars were now full, and the shelves brimming with fresh fruits and plates of delectable delights beckoned.

Peadar rubbed the back of his neck. "We don't have a ton of food on the island at the best of times. I mean, we do okay. But sometimes you get tired of eating the same thing. So I make it look different. And the Lost Boys grumble less. It's all in the mind, you know?"

"You trick them?"

"What? No! They all know it's an illusion."

"Illusion..." she murmured, rubbing her hands over a red apple, its skin reflecting the light. "Can all faeries make magic like that?"

"All faeries have a natural affinity for magic, but our exact talents are unique."

"Peadar's the only one who can do illusions around here," a new voice interrupted, the coldness of the tone driving Cäcilia to edge closer to Peadar.

She turned to see a group of faeries enter, though their features were hard to distinguish thanks to the light behind them. Each held a small circular shield and either a spear or a sword.

"Branwen," Peadar said, his tone flat. "Did you find all the intruders?"

"Three — this one makes four." She smiled at Cäcilia, but there was no warmth in her tone. "Thank you for waylaying her."

"Cäcilia isn't one of them. She's with me."

Branwen's eyes narrowed. "A human, Peadar? They can't be trusted."

"She's under my protection, Branwen," he countered.

Cäcilia wrapped her arms around herself as the other faery drew nearer. Her bronze wings shone, the edges sharp, as if cut from the metal. Branwen was no taller than Cäcilia or Peadar, but she carried herself with a confidence that forced others to look up at her.

"Your protection?" Branwen scoffed. "I think you mean mine."

Cäcilia opened her mouth to protest, but she couldn't find the words. What could she say to this armed warrior faery?

"I am still lord of this island, Branwen," Peadar said, his voice hard.

"And I'm the captain of the guard. And I say humans are a threat."

"She's not. She's not like the others," Peadar countered, his tone firm but defensive, the weight of his words carrying an edge that Cäcilia couldn't decipher.

Branwen took a half step closer. "The last time you trusted a human didn't turn out so well, did it?"

"I'm right this time."

"Who is she?"

"That doesn't matter. I promised her help."

Branwen flicked her gaze from Peadar to Cäcilia and back. "I'll trust you. For now. But it better not be like last time."

With that, she turned on her heel and marched out. The others followed.

Peadar grabbed Cäcilia's hand. "I'm sorry you had to witness that."

"What did she mean, 'last time'?"

He stiffened beside her. "Come on. Let's explore the island now that the intruders are gone."

Chapter Nine

The trees were singing as Peadar guided Cäcilia out of the earthen room under the tree. Branwen and the Lost Boys had left, hopefully to ensure the intruders had returned to the other island.

He didn't expect them to stay there though. An Dorchadas was hardly a welcoming residence, and many would be seeking a way to return home — and that way lay through Never Isle.

"She doesn't like humans much," Cäcilia said.

"Many faeries don't. A lot of humans have come to Tìr nan Òg in recent years, upsetting the balance of faeries and disturbing the natural magic."

"Is that why you don't want those other humans here?"

"They're prisoners, on their own island."

"Is that where Branwen wants to take me? To be locked up with the other humans?"

His chest clenched at the sadness in her voice. He had just rescued her from a prison; he wasn't about to let her go to another. "Not all the intruders are human. All criminals are exiled there. It's not a place we send humans just for being human."

"Oh." Her voice was small, but a sigh of relief filled it.

He pushed aside the horror that she'd thought they locked up all humans just for being different. "Now, where would you like to explore first?"

"Where is the music coming from, please?"

A smile lit up his face. Of course she'd want to know that. Taking her hand in his, all slim and delicate with calloused fingertips, he guided her to a sapling with cream-colored bark and leaves the color of the summer sky. He placed their hands side by side on the trunk. "Do you feel the hum inside?"

She frowned in concentration, a line creasing her pale forehead. "It's like the tree is vibrating."

"That's the magic inside." He pulled a thin branch toward her, the leaves dancing softly in the slight breeze. "And here — feel the leaves."

With light fingers, she brushed over them. "Tiny holes?"

"The wind makes the music by blowing past the holes in the leaves. But the magic in the tree — that vibration — is what keeps the whole thing in tune. If the magic is corrupted in any way, the tree gets out of tune. At first, only certain leaves or branches will be off, and that can be hard to detect. But if it gets bad, it can disrupt the harmony of an entire grove."

Cäcilia leaned forward and blew over a leaf. A gentle note played, making her smile. "What do you do if that happens?"

"Jowan has plant magic, so he can diagnose the problem and often cajole the tree into returning to harmony. But if it's bad enough, the tree may die and have to be removed."

She placed her hand on the trunk. "Poor things. I never heard music like this from the tower. Was I just too far away?"

Peadar laughed. "No, Tìr nan Òg has many magical plants, but the singing trees are unique to Never Isle. Come on, I've so much more to show you!"

He grabbed her hand and lifted them into the air.

"Peadar!" she screamed. "What are you doing?"

"Showing you my home?" He slowed their ascent, turning to face her.

"You can't just grab me and take off! I'm not a bag of apples!"

Oh. His ears flamed. "You're right. I'm so sorry. Would you like to return to the ground?"

She took a deep breath, mollified. "No, we can continue. But please...ask before you do that? It's very disconcerting, and all the colors blend together and make me dizzy."

Guilt washed over him. "I'll do better, I promise." He tightened his grip on her hand. "Are you ready to see the Great Tree?"

"Yes, please."

With a more sedate pace, he flew them in an ascending circle around the tree that reached to the heavens. Giant branches stretched out at increasing intervals, and more faeries flew in and out of carved doors. He lighted on a branch that was not quite as wide as his wings and ensured Cäcilia stood firmly before releasing her hand. A worn path flattened the top of the branch, making walking easy, but like the other faeries, he kept his wings outstretched to help with balance. Knowing Cäcilia wouldn't have that option, he walked slowly toward the trunk, her hand on his shoulder to guide her.

Sounds of laughter and merriment spilled out of the arch to greet them. A buzzing ball of light zipped past their heads as they entered, and a call of apology broke over the general cacophony.

"What is this place?" Cäcilia asked, her voice raised to be heard.

"Our main hall," he replied, waving a hand at the large space.

The hollow in the tree was as high as it was wide, with lots of room for the faeries to hover over the furniture that was scattered around the room. Two large tables sprawled across the middle, at angles to each other. Chairs of all shapes and sizes and varying degrees of comfort gathered in small groups or stood alone in pockets of space.

Faeries lounged around, some tinkering at things, others playing games. All of them seemed to be talking at once. Cäcilia shifted closer to him, and he put a protective arm around her. He led her away from the worst of the chaos to a couple of chairs by one of the tables.

Peadar handed Cäcilia a mug of juice made from the purple berries that grew all over the glade. She took an appreciative sip and settled into the chair, pushing her heavy braid to one side.

"How many Lost Boys are there?" she asked. "And why do you call them that?"

He sipped his own beverage to hide his embarrassment. He'd been the one to name them when he first arrived, but he now felt bad for the implications it carried. Nonetheless, the faeries had claimed their lost status, and the name had stuck. "I've lost count of how many of us there are now. But this is home for many faeries who felt out of place or had nowhere else to go."

"What about Branwen? She's not a boy."

"No, she was the first girl, actually. She and her brothers, Jowan and Maelore, found the first path through the fogs along the coast to get here. But the boys hid her at first, so I thought there weren't any girls around."

She started to ask him something else, then stopped, her head tilted. "A violin!" She leapt to her feet and moved toward the sound. He followed, shaking his head that she could hear it through the continuing chaos. He heard nothing like the music she had played when he first found her.

They wove their way through the chairs, under an aerial game of keep-away, and passed a mock sword fight.

She paused before a small faery sitting cross-legged on the floor. He held the instrument across his lap and plucked at the strings one at a time. With a deft lift of her skirt, she settled on the floor before the boy and held out her hand.

"May I try?" she asked. "I can show you how to play it."

"No!" cried the boy. "It's my fidhle!"

"Of course it is. I just want to help."

"Let her try it, Maelore," Peter encouraged.

Somewhat mollified, the boy let her lift it from his lap. She held it gently, her hand touching the bridge and the tuning pegs with care. "Do you have the bow? The long stick that would have been with it?"

The boy shook his head. "Eoinan took it to play swords."

At Cäcilia's cry of horror, Peadar lifted off the ground, angling directly for the two boys who were fighting. He dodged between them, grabbing Eoinan's hand before the long, slender piece of wood could connect with his side.

"That's not a sword!" he cried roughly, reaching for it.

But the younger faery leaned back out of his reach. "You'll have to chase me for it, then!" he cried, backflipping over the heads of those below him.

Peadar tore after him, his wings a blur of green. The two zipped around the room, knocking over games, upsetting chairs, and narrowly avoiding colliding with others as they leapt out of the way. Peadar laughed at the challenge as Eoinan mocked him. Soon, everyone below was involved, cheering or jeering as the chase continued. The thrill of the flight filled Peadar, and he began throwing up illusions to disorient Eoinan.

The younger faery darted around a stack of books, knocking one over. The bow caught the edge of the book with an odd twang.

Peadar threw up another illusion to disorient Eoinan, forcing the boy to tumble toward the ceiling.

"Enough!" The cry ripped through the noise, and Peadar nearly spun into a wall before he could stop himself.

Cäcilia was standing on a chair, hands on her hips. "What are you doing, all of you? That is a valuable part of the instrument, and you've nearly destroyed it!"

Chagrinned, Peadar returned to the ground. Eoinan flew over to Cäcilia and handed her the bow with lowered head. She accepted it gracefully, and patted his shoulder. She turned to get down but faltered.

In an instance, Peadar was by her side, offering his hand. She took it, but she still wouldn't look him in the eye.

"I'm sorry?" he offered.

"You know what your problem is, Peadar? You don't think."

His heart sank at having disappointed her twice in one day.

Even worse was the glare Branwen was sending his way from where she lurked just inside the arch.

Chapter Ten

Cäcilia stood among the silent faeries, her heart pounding. What had possessed her to shout at them like that? They *were* behaving like children, but shouting was hardly the answer.

But they were all still staring at her, expecting...something. The glint of bronze against the wall told her that Branwen had witnessed her outburst. She drew in a breath, lifting her chin. If they were waiting for her to say something, very well.

"That's enough tomfoolery from all of you. It's time to clean up this mess and get to work."

A flurry of protests broke out, but she held up her hand to silence it. "Clean it up, or no music for you."

The faeries looked at one another, then slowly turned away to do her bidding. Peadar stayed by her side, and for a moment, she thought about sending him to help too, but that would mean she would be alone, and she wasn't ready to brave Branwen by herself.

"I'm sorry we upset you."

She sighed at yet another apology from him and rubbed her head at the sudden ache. "I'd like to go outside."

He tucked her hand in his arm and guided her through the chairs, for once not taking to the air. Branwen didn't move as they walked past her, and Cäcilia didn't take the time to study her face to read her expression.

She closed her eyes against the glare of the sun, pulling to a stop while she adjusted to the change in light. Peadar waited quietly, then led her around the side of the tree, following a narrow ledge she hadn't noticed before. At the elbow of another branch was a wider spot, with a seat fashioned into it. She sank into it, careful of the damaged bow. Lifting it to the light, she ran her fingers over it, feeling for damage. Other than a few nicks in the tip, she found nothing to be concerned about. The hair hadn't fared so well, pieces of it hanging down in long ribbons. There was nothing she could do about that now, but even ignoring that, she was missing one key element that she needed to play.

"Rosin," she murmured.

"What's that?" Peadar asked.

"I need rosin or tree sap in order to play."

He thrust something into her hands and took off in an instant.

The violin. He'd brought the violin with him. A smile lifted the corners of her mouth. He might be impulsive at times, but Peadar did notice the important things. She set the bow aside for the moment and explored the violin. It was horribly out of tune and scuffed, but it still had a good sound. She raised it to her chin and plucked a string, adjusting the pegs till she was happy with the note it produced, then repeated the process with each of them.

A green figure rose up toward her and lighted on the branch. Peadar grinned at her as he held out a leaf, panting from his haste. "I asked Jowan to purify it, so it shouldn't be dirty."

She smiled in surprise that he would have thought of that as she took the leaf from him.

"I guessed why you wanted it, and having bits of bark in the rosin didn't seem like a good idea."

"Thank you. That will make a difference." She handed him the violin and lifted the bow, finding the start of the hair with her fingers, though staying careful not to touch the fine fibers. She ran the cleansed sap along the bow in smooth strokes. After some time, she set it aside.

"I think that's the best I can do for now. The horsehair will need to be replaced at some point, though it should be usable now."

Eagerly Peadar held out the violin to her. "Will you play, then?"

The hope in his voice was hard to deny, and a warmth spread up her neck as she accepted the instrument. Tucking it under her chin, she tested the bow and the tuning with a series of light notes, like a brook tripping over rocks in the forest.

A rustling sound made her look up. All around, faeries were hurrying to find places along the nearby branches, pushing and whispering to one another.

"She's going to play it!"

"But it's mine." This from little Maelore.

"Shush so we can hear."

Cäcilia lowered the violin. "Lost Boys, did you finish tidying the living space?" She nodded at one of the young women, acknowledging the usage of the group name.

"We did!" came the chorus of replies.

"And you're going to sit quietly so everyone can hear?"

Again, they called in agreement.

"Very well."

She began playing once more, closing her eyes to focus on the music. Starting with a simple run of scales, she thought about what to play, remembering her last attempt at capturing flight. But that had been before she'd flown herself.

Remembering the way the wind had tugged her hair, the weightlessness, the freedom of flight while holding Peadar's hand, she let it flow through her hand to the bow, to the strings. She thought of the storm, the exhilaration of racing the rain. The beauty of the glen. The peaceful forest, followed by the foggy sea.

Her body swayed as she played, her eyes closed as she focused on the moment. A smile danced over her mouth as she thought about the faeries tumbling and chasing each other through the air. Her bow picked up speed as she added notes and built on the melody, spinning it around on itself, only to lift higher and higher, as if reaching for the heavens.

At last her arm grew tired, and she shifted to a slower yet whimsical melody as she guided her listeners back to that moment under the tree. The last note faded on the wind as she opened her eyes.

The branches were even more full of the bright-colored lumps she knew to be the faeries. All at once, the air filled with a great rustling sound as each of the lumps began to glow. She turned to Peadar to ask what was happening and gasped in awe.

He stood before her, his toes just brushing the branch. His wings were a blur of glowing green light. The grin on his face told her everything. But the wonder in his eyes made her heart race. She swallowed hard, a blush creeping over her cheeks. She turned away to rest the violin on a safe ledge before loosening the bow.

The faeries drifted away to return to their duties, and Peadar gathered the violin and bow and followed Maelore inside to find the case or somewhere safe to store it, as the little boy was still insisting it belonged to him.

A shadow fell across Cäcilia, and she looked up to see Branwen hovering nearby.

"You did well," the faery said, albeit somewhat begrudgingly.

"Thank you."

"I mean it. The Lost Boys are...lost. You handled them well. And the music... I've not heard anything like that since I was a girl."

Cäcilia nodded, unsure of what to say.

A war cry echoed across the island.

Chapter Eleven

Mara's wings shimmered a deep purple as she flew through the fog. The barrier around An Dorchadas felt wrong, but she didn't have time to fix it. She could only hope that it would recognize her and let her pass through.

A teasing wind tugged at her skirt, testing to see if she'd give in, but she brushed it aside. If her suspicions were correct, then she needed to reach the island quickly.

What fool, that human, being caught and sent here.

If he'd only listened to her, he would still be where she had placed him. She could only hope he was still able to provide her with some assistance.

He owed her that much at least.

The barrier grew stronger, pushing against her. Someone else had tried to reinforce it. If it were her magic, it wouldn't work on her. It didn't work on anyone once they realized it was an illusion.

And this was. Whether created by her or someone else, the only way for this much fog to exist was for it not to.

With that knowledge, the swirling clouds fell away before her, revealing a perfectly circular island around a conical volcano. Dormant, of course. Even she wasn't evil enough to send prisoners to be killed by an active one.

A ship lay at anchor off the eastern coast. The starboard list was less pronounced than before, she noted. And several of the prisoners were working about the deck.

So. They'd found a way to reach the ship.

The man she was looking for was on the bridge. Of course he was. He paced the small deck, shouting at the others. His clothes were better than the rest, but they still showed signs of wear. No magically renewing clothing here. She flew down, landing on the deck behind him.

He started at the slight thump as she stretched her wings after her rushed flight.

"What are you doing here?" he sneered.

"Is that any way to greet your queen?" She flexed her hands. "After I came all this way to see you?"

"You want something." He leaned against the railing, crossing his arms.

She swallowed back a retort at his obvious disrespect. Now was not the time to be petulant. "Of course I do. Ours has ever been a transactional relationship. Why would it change now?"

"Good," he said, leaning forward. "Because I'm going to make you pay for your favor."

Her jaw clenched as she fought not to react. "Why such hostility? We were friends for so long."

"Friends?" he scoffed. "Why should I trust you after everything you did?"

Ah, there it was. She offered him a tight-lipped smirk. "Because, my dear boy, I can get you off this island."

He jerked, then relaxed, but it was too late. She knew she had him.

"And what must I do to earn this pardon?"

Ha. As if she'd pardon him for failing her so badly. But he didn't need to know the details. "I need your help finding someone."

"In case you hadn't noticed, I'm rather trapped here." He waved a sweeping arm at the volcano.

She cocked her head. "Are you? A little birdy told me you'd found a way to...stretch your boundaries."

"And if that's true?"

She'd had enough of his games. "A girl in my care has been kidnapped, and I have reason to believe that she's been taken to Never Isle."

It was his turn to look superior. "The one place you can't go in all of Tìr nan Òg."

As much as it irritated her, the fact was not a secret. She didn't bother responding.

He pushed off the railing and walked to the other side of the deck. "Who is she?"

"That is none of your concern."

He paused in front of her, a triumphant look hiding in his eyes. "Oh, it is if you want my help."

"A human who has been in my care for some time. She will be unfamiliar with her surroundings, easily lost."

He stepped nearer, into her personal space. She was tall for a faery, and he was short for a human, so they were of about equal stature. She held her ground...and her breath until he stepped back.

"I want your word I'll be released."

"You already have it."

"And my men."

"One man."

"And five hundred pieces of gold."

"That's enough," she snapped, turning to leave. She would not entertain his folly any longer.

He laughed. "See you, Mara," he mocked, sweeping a bow.

She narrowed her eyes in return. "Phillip."

Chapter Twelve

Peadar's head snapped up as the eerie cry reverberated around the glen. He shoved the violin into Maelore's hands and ripped out the door.

"Stay down!" he shouted to Cäcilia, hoping she'd remain tucked into the ledge of the tree and go unnoticed.

He darted through the air, throwing up a rock wall illusion as he went. Unfortunately, some of the intruders had already passed it, spiraling up out of the way.

Below, Jowan slipped to the edge of the glade, where four key trees were planted close together. From there, his magic would be able to flow through the other trees.

Branwen had her squad encircling the intruders on the ground, her staff raised to fend off the attack from a squat human in a striped shirt.

Confident that everyone was right where they should be, Peadar dodged to cut off a group of faeries intent on getting past the great tree. One of them shot a bolt of light at him, but he deflected it back while pulling an illusion of giant magpies from the higher branches. The three faeries broke apart, coming at him from different directions.

He twisted and spun through the air, exhilaration thrilling through him as he led them on a chase through the trees. A branch reached out and wrapped itself around one of the faeries, plucking her from the sky. Peadar waved his thanks to Jowan and headed for the lagoon, the other two hot on his heels. He laughed as he flew.

The prisoners must not escape, he knew that, but it had been far too long since he had flown like this, with every fiber of his being honed for battle. Another bolt of light flashed behind him, and he rolled out of the way just in time.

Flying on his back, he watched the faeries chasing him. He had no idea what their crimes were. He was never told.

But he had been placed in charge of keeping the prisoners exiled on the volcanic island for a reason.

Because he was the best.

Folding his wings, he dropped from the sky, letting gravity speed his descent. Above, the two were slow to follow his sudden change of direction, but once they spotted him, they sped after. A playful grin crossed his face. They wouldn't reach him in time.

He fluttered his wings slightly. A hand's breadth above the shimmering water, he flattened out, flying with his toes skimming the surface. A cackling cry broke from his lips as he darted through a series of rocks.

A splash sounded behind him as one of the other faeries couldn't stop in time.

Two down.

The other faery was clever, staying just far enough back to avoid Peadar's tricks. But not for long. Peadar returned to the trees, using his speed and knowledge of the forest to rip in and out of the narrowest of spaces.

His pursuer was almost as fast and rose above the canopy to follow. Peadar mounted to the sky to face him. He noted with surprise that they were almost to the farthest edge of the island, and for a moment, concern flashed through him.

But for now, he had to put this faery in his place.

The sun beat down around him, the sky above a perfect lilac. Another bolt of light zoomed at him. He curved his body up and over it, sending it away with his magic.

"There's no shadows here, Peadar," called the other faery, one he now recognized as being among the oldest residents of An Dorchadas — and one of the few who knew about Peadar's second magical ability.

The ability that gave him the advantage over most other faeries.

The reason Mara had named him lord of the Never Isles.

Shadow magic.

More light blasted at him, and he spun away to avoid being hit.

If anyone asked, he said he had light magic, because in many ways it was the same. To most everyone, it seemed he could control light, but in reality, it was the shadow he manipulated that moved the light.

But the other faery was right. Above the canopy, nothing blocked the sunlight. Peadar cast an illusion of clouds that dimmed the light, but it was not enough to form a shadow.

Changing tactics, he drew his sword and darted directly toward his opponent.

A furious battle ensued, neither of them gaining much on the other. He used his sword as a distraction to keep the faery from throwing more light at him as he slowly drew them to the trees. When at last he was close enough, he threw an illusion of fluffkins at the faery. As the other faery dodged out of the way of the snarling creatures, Peadar pulled the shadows from the branches and twisted them around his legs and wings, until he was trapped in the shade of the trees.

"Ha! I won!" he crowed, triumph flowing through him. He felt invincible, and he threw his head back to catch his breath.

"Have you?" asked the faery with a knowing grin. "You caught me, but that's hardly winning the battle."

Fear coursed through Peadar. How could he have been so foolish? He sped away through the trees, one thought spurring him onward: Cäcilia.

The glade was in shambles when he reached it. Branwen battled four humans on her own, her squad nowhere in sight. Smaller trees had been uprooted. Wounded faeries from both sides limped away. The noise was a muffled roar that beat against him.

And Cäcilia stood on the great branch overlooking the glen, violin in hand. Her hair streamed out behind her, fluttering in the wind that twisted through the glade. She raised the instrument, her bow slicing across the strings like a sword. The opening notes were bold and unrelenting — a furious cascade of rapid strokes that echoed the chaos around her, each string vibrating with the urgency of clashing swords and beating wings.

The noise of the battle paused as everyone looked up. Then the music flowed through them, and the Lost Boys renewed their efforts against the intruders.

Peadar's exhaustion fell away, and he darted down to join the battle. Branwen nodded her appreciation, her staff tripping up one of the humans. Together, they pushed the group back toward the trail that led to the shore, and the men turned and ran.

Movement caught his eye, and he glanced through the trees to see someone watching. There was a familiarity about him that Peadar couldn't place. The newest prisoner wasn't fighting. He leaned against one of the trunks with casual grace, unconcerned when he knew he'd been spotted. He raised a makeshift sword to his forehead in a mock salute. With a final glance at the home tree, the prisoner turned and walked away. Shortly after, the rest of the prisoners followed, herded along by the Lost Boys.

Peadar sank to his knees in the center of the glade, ignoring the mud that stained his trousers. Above him, Cäcilia's music shifted to more peaceful strains before fading to a close.

She's magnificent, he thought as a strange feeling coursed through him. Not many people would be able to go from living in a secluded tower to having the presence of mind to play in the midst of battle.

"Where did you go?" demanded Branwen, interrupting his thoughts.

"Leading away some of the prisoners," he retorted.

"You took them back to An Dorchadas?" she asked in surprise.

"No, I —" He spun back to the trees where the strange human had stood, then looked back at Cäcilia.

"They weren't trying to escape," he whispered.

Chapter Thirteen

Cäcilia's hands trembled as she lowered her bow. The cacophony of the battle was over, but the damage remained. Branwen called for a headcount, and Cäcilia sagged with relief when she heard Peadar's reply. She couldn't say for sure why she had picked up the violin to play, but the music in the trees had called to her. She'd found the out-of-sync tones and guided them back to one chorus that seemed to energize the Lost Boys.

Eoinan's shout beside her nearly made her stumble off the limb. She turned as he unfurled his wings. "Will you take me down there with you?"

He nodded, grabbing her hand as he lifted from the branch. As the forest floor came into focus, Cäcilia winced at the devastation. Broken trees, discarded weapons, injured faeries. Her feet settled onto the torn-up grass. All around, faeries were attending to their duties, helping to clean up the glade.

"How can I help?" she asked. But Eoinan was already gone.

She looked around, peering through the dwindling light. Dim shapes moved about as the injured were being carried over to the base of the tree. With careful steps, she crossed to the Great Tree. She stowed the violin in the dugout Peadar had shown her only a few short hours ago and filled a pitcher of water.

With the handles of several cups looped over her other hand, she headed for the injured faeries. Water splashed over her hand as she stumbled over a root.

"Careful," called a voice to her left, and as she spun around to avoid them, her foot caught on another root. The cups tumbled to the ground as she tried to catch herself, clutching the pitcher to her. A hand wrapped around her arm, pulling her up.

The Lost Boy gave her a pitying look as he helped her gain her balance, then took the water from her.

Chastened, she returned to the tree, sliding her feet over the ground to avoid tripping again. The front of her dress was damp. *Foolish girl,* she scolded herself, the voice in her head sounding a lot like Amaran. *How can you expect to help them when you can't even see?*

Her fingers twitched as if holding the bow, but she pushed aside the urge to find comfort in the violin. Music was hardly a help. Her playing had merely been a distraction for the intruders.

Branwen's commanding voice cut through the glade, pulling her from her thoughts. "We have one," she called.

Cäcilia squinted through the growing haze. Two Lost Boys dragged a human prisoner out of the trees. He was taller than the faeries, but rail thin, his clothes hanging off his lean frame. She edged closer, staying out of the way of the faeries, but she was curious about another human. To her shock, his hair was short and spiky. For some reason, she had half expected his hair to be as long as hers. None of the faeries had extraordinarily long hair, so she thought long hair might have been a human trait.

"Why are you here?" Branwen asked the prisoner, her voice sharp.

"Freedom, obviously," the human replied, spitting at the guard's feet. "We've spent quite long enough rotting on that forsaken rock, and we're ready to go home."

"Why come through Never Isle if you want freedom?"

"Because everyone knows the barrier is weaker here. Getting to Tìr nan Òg from An Dorchadas is impossible."

"How did you get from An Dorchadas to here?"

He leaned forward, glaring up at Branwen. "Wouldn't you like to know?"

The faery barely moved, nothing more than a twist of her hand. The man crumbled backward with a cry of pain. "Fine! I'll tell you!"

Whatever Branwen had done ended, for the man stopped shouting and instead lay panting for a moment. Branwen nudged him with her staff. Cäcilia hesitated, wanting to pull away, yet the need to see drew her closer.

"The barrier around An Dorchadas has also weakened. We've been trying to get through it, but it's not enough to reach the mainland. But it is enough to reach here."

A shiver ran over Cäcilia as she processed his words. If the barrier was weak, then all the prisoners could escape.

"So why not just sneak through?" Branwen continued her interrogation. "Why start the fight?"

He scoffed. "Like you would have just let us through."

"Some of you would have made it."

"You're right. But he's got a plan, doesn't he? Needed us to do that, see."

"Why?"

"Said we had to pick up a few things along the way," he sneered. He shifted, and even without seeing him clearly, Cäcilia could somehow feel his eyes on her.

A moment passed, and then understanding washed over her. She stumbled back with a gasp, her hair catching on a root. She tugged it free as she spun away.

Straight into something solid.

Peadar grunted as his arms slipped around her. "I've got you."

Relief washed over her. He was here.

"Come away," he said, bending down to untangle her hair, then tucking her hand under his elbow. "Branwen will handle the prisoners."

"Isn't that your job?" she asked.

He hesitated. "Yes and no. Branwen is in charge of security. I maintain the magic around the islands and ensure the overall safety of the Lost Boys."

She followed him toward the sound of a crackling fire, and he helped her get comfortable on one of the logs nearby. Jowan passed them bowls of food, and Cäcilia dug in, surprised at how hungry she was.

"I'm sorry my illusions won't help you much," Peadar said as he poked at his own serving.

"But it's delicious," she told him. "I'm not a very good cook, so I tend to just munch on vegetables raw."

He shifted to sit cross-legged on the log. "Well, *I* am a great cook, you know —"

A snort of laughter from across the fire cut him off.

"I am," he continued. "I just don't like to show up the others, so I let them take turns."

"Of course you are," she replied over the scoffs from the Lost Boys. "So kind to not flaunt your skills."

"Exactly."

Their teasing turned to other topics, but a warmth settled in Cäcilia's stomach. She'd never known such a pleasant evening. Despite the attack and her worry for Amaran, the company of the faeries had been nice. And Peadar... Peadar was far kinder than she had dreamed someone could be.

"Are you ready to turn in?" he asked.

She glanced up at the tree, remembering the chaotic events of her first foray inside. Her consternation must have shown on her face, because he laughed.

"We don't all sleep in the main room. We have smaller living spaces. You could have your own room."

That was almost worse. "May I sleep in the dugout?"

He hesitated. "Yes...but why?"

She tugged on her hair. "I can't fly. What if I get up in the night and can't see where I'm going and fall?"

He claimed her hand again. "I would never let that happen. But I see your point."

With their fingers still intertwined, he led her to the entrance of the dugout and helped her step down into the dim space. Tiredness washed over her, and she swayed as she walked, content to let him warn her of any hazards. Why was it that she trusted him so implicitly?

She couldn't say for sure. She just knew that she did.

He showed her the inner room with several bunks. "This is the girls' side. The boys sleep across the way. Blankets are in the trunk here, and anything else you might need is in the bureau. I'll leave the lantern, if you like?"

"You can take it," she said with a small smile. "I'm too tired, and it's just a glare I can't see beyond right now."

"Oh, sorry."

"It's fine."

He shifted closer, his hand brushing her arm. Her heart raced, and she wondered if he could hear it. Was he...? Did she want him to...?

He stepped back before she could even decide what question to form. "Good night, Cäcilia," he whispered, then he was gone.

She shivered in his absence, the strangeness of the room suddenly wrapping around her. With her hand held out in front of her, she counted her steps to the bureau and dug through the drawers until she found a nightgown that would fit her. She washed up with the water in a bowl on the top that Peadar had filled. A few more cautious steps to the trunk with the blankets. She fell into the nearest bunk and pulled the blanket over herself.

As she drifted off to sleep, the sounds of the others outside slowly faded, until only the hum of the tree remained — a hum that refused to resonate with the rest of the forest.

Chapter Fourteen

Peadar made his way back to the makeshift campfire. With so many of the faeries injured on the ground, Thalion had started the triage there rather than in the infirmary near the top of the tree. The comforting fire offered a gathering place for the faeries while their wounds could be addressed or the more injured were flown up to heal for the night.

Part of him desperately wanted to carry Cäcilia as high as he could to protect her from the humans. But she had chosen the option she had control over, and he couldn't blame her. If she fell from the tree, he would never forgive himself.

He hung the lantern on a branch and flexed his hand, the feel of hers still lingering. He thought of her gray eyes, her impossibly long hair. The little red mark on her jaw where it rested against the violin. She trusted him. Trusted him enough to leave her home. To lift her off the ground and fly. To be her eyes.

He didn't deserve her trust.

A spear appeared in his path to block him, the handle smacking against his chest. His wings flared out for balance, their green glow lighting up the trees around him.

Glaring, he spun to see Branwen giving him a pointed look from her seat on a log. "What was that for?"

She nodded at his feet.

Oh.

He'd nearly tripped over another log that had been dragged near the fire. "Uh, thank you," he said as he stepped around it to take a seat. He let his wings fade from sight again.

"What's got your head full of clouds?" she asked.

"Nothing."

"I'm sure 'nothing' has a name and hair that can wrap around the base of the tree, but we have more important things to talk about."

His shoulders deflated as she gave him an out, so he didn't have to deny that he'd been thinking about Cäcilia. "What is so important then?"

"The barrier."

Inwardly, he groaned. "It's not my fault," he protested.

She shook her head. "I'm not saying it is. But you are distracted."

"They can't expect me to stay here forever and not make friends."

She flinched. "You have plenty of friends. Friends are not the problem."

"You know what I mean."

"I know you made a promise."

He flung a stone into the fire. "A promise that makes me little better than the prisoners. *I'm* a prisoner."

She gave him a look of something almost like pity.

"What?" he snapped.

"Lord of the Never Isles was a title you earned, and quite proudly, if I remember correctly."

Heat seared his face, and not from the fire. "Can't a faery repent?"

"Repent, yes. But the punishment remains. What you did..."

"Was horrible, I know." He cut her off.

"Was a mistake," she continued, ignoring his interruption. "The high council can't revoke the title. Only Mara can."

He gave a scoffing laugh. "As if she ever would."

"You're right; she won't. And do you know why?"

"Because she needs a jailer?"

"Because you're too powerful."

"She might have to find two people to take the position, you mean."

"No — she doesn't want to risk facing you as an adversary."

"My magic isn't that powerful."

"You have no idea how powerful it is because you're too busy behaving like a lark to test your limits."

His fist clenched involuntarily. "Branwen..." he warned.

"No, you listen, Peadar. You've had it easy. The prisoners were locked behind the barrier, and all you had to do was make sure they stayed there. No other responsibilities. So you never grew up. You've spent years sulking."

"You know what happened," he ground out.

"I know you chose what seemed easiest at the time."

"*Enough!*" he roared, leaping to his feet. His magic swirled around him, causing the flames to flicker wildly.

The gasp that followed wasn't Branwen's. As one, they spun toward the undergrowth.

Wide, panicked eyes locked onto his, framed by a pale face streaked with dirt and sweat.

Peadar leaped up to race after the prisoner.

A war cry broke out as the humans and exiles poured from the darkness.

Peadar called on his magic, but he was too distracted for it to respond properly.

How did they get across with no warning?

A piercing scream ripped through him.

Cäcilia.

He was in the air before he even stopped to think about it, racing toward the burrow. All around him, the glade lit up as faeries let their wings shine from the magic they poured out. Arrows darted all around him, nicking his clothing and forcing him to fly higher to thwart their trajectories.

"*Peadar!*"

Her desperate voice cut through the sounds of battle, piercing his heart worse than any of the arrows could have done. He flipped over a thick branch, letting the projectiles hit the tree.

Gravity joined with the strength of his wings as he dove for the entrance to the burrow.

Light from the burrow's open door spilled out into the night. Two men ran for the trees, hauling Cäcilia between them.

He called her name, and she turned toward him, her grey eyes wide and filled with panic.

"Peadar!" She jerked one arm free, reaching up to grasp his own.

Searing pain shot through his left wing. He spun around, slamming into the trunk of the Great Tree. Rough bark scraped against his face.

Cäcilia's screams faded as darkness swooped over him.

Chapter Fifteen

C ool, rough stone pressed against her cheek. Cäcilia forced her eyes open, but only darkness greeted her. Her heart raced as she fought the rising panic until the truth set in. She couldn't see because no light reached the depths of the cave she was in, not because her vision had failed completely.

She held tight to that knowledge and focused on her other senses. She'd already decided she was in a cave. The lack of light was only one clue, combined with the way the slightest sounds echoed back at her. A musty smell added to her conclusion, though a light draft assured her there was a way out.

Shifting, she moved her arms to push herself upright, but ropes around her wrists impeded the movement. Scratchiness in her throat threatened to turn into a sob.

Where was Peadar?

He had been there when she was taken. She'd heard him. Had seen him — at least, she was convinced she had seen the green glow of his wings as he sped toward her. The last of the memory formed in her mind, and this time, she couldn't stop the sob. Something had hit him, and he had fallen from the sky, his wings flickering out.

No, Peadar wouldn't be coming to rescue her.

But Peadar or no, she couldn't stay in the cave. She lifted her bound wrists to her mouth and bit into the coarse rope. After a few minutes of tugging, her hands grew heavy and her fingers thick.

She'd pulled the wrong piece and inadvertently tightened the knots. In frustration, she let her hands fall, hoping the blood would start to circulate again.

How was she going to get out of this mess? Living her entire life locked in a tower had taught her no skills for how to survive or fend for herself. All she'd had was her music and her books.

Books.

The literature Amaran had managed to scrounge for her had been eclectic and haphazard at best. One of the stranger books she'd brought home had been on shiphandling. A lot of complex math and star charts had challenged her, and she probably should have questioned why none of the constellations had ever appeared in the sky over her tower. But it also had contained a large section on knots.

She tugged at the rope again, her teeth finding the ridges between the strands. She concentrated on the shape of the knot, trying to identify which one it might be. Fibers filled her mouth, and she spat them to the side.

Recalling the books made her think of Amaran. Had her guardian returned to the tower to find it damaged and Cäcilia missing? Was she worried? Was she even now searching for her? Guilt pressed against her. She had put aside her quest of finding Amaran to enjoy time with Peadar, exploring a world she had only witnessed from afar.

Her teeth slipped on the rope and she bit down hard on her lip. Pain brought tears to her eyes, and she was tempted to give in to the despair. She curled up in a ball, her still-bound wrists hugging her knees to her chest. Her thin nightdress did little to keep her warm, and she pulled it down over her bare toes.

Unbidden, Amaran's voice filled her mind. "Fear clouds the mind. Use your head, not your heart."

Why the stern guardian had thought a girl trapped in a tower needed that advice, she'd never known. But Amaran had felt it applied to many things in life. Not giving up on her music practice. Learning to navigate the tower with her fading vision. Cooking for herself.

Amaran had left her alone ever since she had been a young girl. Why hadn't Cäcilia realized that was unusual sooner? The faery had hidden the fact that she was different from the girl, but she'd never claimed the title of "mother." She'd learned about family units from her books.

Books that she would pour over for two or three months, gleaning everything she could from them until they would vanish and Amaran would bring new ones to replace them.

Was Amaran *returning* the books? If so, then where had she gotten them?

So many questions Cäcilia was ashamed she had never thought to ask before.

Her movements stilled. What was the point in escaping when she didn't know where to go next? Her heart cried to return to Peadar, but her head said that was foolish, and that she should return to Amaran instead. But could she trust the woman who had locked her away and lied to her for her entire life?

And why had she locked her in a tower like a prisoner?

Chapter Sixteen

"Peadar!"

From her tone, Branwen had clearly been shouting at him for a while. He sat up, shaking his head to rid himself of the tinny bells ringing in his ears.

A mistake.

The bells turned to buzzing, and he retched.

"Ugh. You better not have gotten that on my boots," Branwen complained.

"Thank you for your consideration," he retorted, glaring up at her. A blue glow lit up his usual chamber. It felt wrong, but he couldn't place why.

She handed him a rag and a water pouch. "I woke you up, didn't I?"

The way his head was pounding, he wasn't sure it was the favor she implied. "You're too kind."

"They took the girl."

His stomach lurched, and he clamped a hand over his mouth to keep from retching again — thankfully the one with the rag and not the water pouch. "Where is she?"

"If I knew that, I wouldn't have bothered waking you."

She waited for him to have a swig of water before holding out a leaf. He eyed it a minute, weighing the benefits versus the horrid taste he knew it held.

"They're not on Never Isle any longer."

Branwen's continued report convinced him, and he grabbed the leaf to chew on. The bitterness flowed over his tongue, but his stomach calmed almost immediately.

"I need to go after her," Peadar said as he chewed.

"Yep."

"Why are you in my room?" Perhaps not the most pressing question, but he was missing something, he was sure of it.

"You hit your head pretty hard, so we brought you up here to heal."

He squinted up at her. "You healed me."

She turned her head away. "Yes."

He let that wash over him. All faeries had the ability to help heal others, while some had true healing magic. Branwen's magic was unique and powerful; she could channel it into almost any form she wanted, but it left her drained and weak for long periods after.

Now that his head had stopped spinning, he could see more clearly. She wasn't standing over him like he'd thought. She perched on a stool, leaning against her staff to keep herself upright.

"You're a fool," he said fondly as he got to his feet, ignoring the way the world tilted. "Why?"

"You were right — there's something special about her."

"I didn't —"

Branwan cut him off with a scoff. "I don't mean like that. I mean, if the exiles are willing to attack us twice, and delay their escape by taking her, something else is going on. She's not just another human lured into Tìr nan Òg."

Peadar ignored the squirmy feeling that crawled up his spine at that comment. "She said her guardian was named Amaran," he shared. He helped himself to another of the bitter leaves to quell his churning stomach.

"You don't think..."

"I didn't, at first. Coincidence of names...but her tower was near where Mara's castle would be. Of course, she'd have it hidden under illusions, so hard to know for sure."

"You think Mara told the girl her name is Amaran?"

He shrugged. "It fits. There was evidence of illusion magic around the tower."

"You can't let her go back to her."

"I don't plan on it."

Branwen swayed, her knuckles white as she clung to her staff. He helped her to lay down, then stepped out of the hollow of the tree. His head and stomach still protested, but he couldn't delay any longer.

Night still wrapped the island in darkness, the stars above flickering purple and orange. He could hear the Lost Boys talking as they patrolled from the air or stood watch. The fire from earlier had dimmed to a pile of red embers in the middle of the glade.

His wings flared out behind him, a dull ache marking the spot where the arrow had ripped through. He swooped down, beckoning the Lost Boys to gather around. A plan was forming in his mind, but he wasn't sure it would work.

But if even Branwen was willing to sacrifice to rescue Cäcilia, then he had to at least try. She was right. No human girl deserved to be held captive, especially not by Mara, the queen of Tìr nan Òg.

Chapter Seventeen

T he queen of Tìr nan Òg was feeling decidedly unqueenly at that particular moment.

The human usurper — who, she might add, had been removed from his stolen throne — was daring to hold *her* captive for ransom.

"We already agreed to the terms," she sneered.

"My men got hurt during the endeavor."

"That's on them for performing the task so poorly."

"We could have escaped, but we did this out of the goodness of our heart, for you. And now we're back where we started."

"You and I both know you wouldn't have been able to escape. You'd have had to defeat the lord of the Never Isles first."

"My scouts report that he was injured during the attack. So you see, we could have overpowered him. But for you, we came back here, with the girl."

Mara's hand tightened. He spoke of her with no more regard than he would one of the haggises that hopped around the hills. "She's not yours to keep," she bit out.

"She's not yours either, is she?" he taunted. "And that's the crux of it, isn't it?"

"Don't meddle with what you don't understand," she warned.

"Oh, I understand plenty. She's leverage. And based on her age and how long she seems to have lived in Tìr nan Òg, I'd wager she's the lost princess of Toricia, isn't she?"

Mara clenched her jaw, not wanting to give anything away to this usurper.

He smirked. "I thought so. Which means you've allowed the war between them and Elpida to continue for more than a decade. My, my, how you enjoy creating havoc among the humans."

"Havoc is your territory, human," she couldn't resist saying.

"Well, borders have never stopped you before, have they?"

"Hand her over," she ordered, tired of the game.

"No."

Something in his eyes flickered, confirming her suspicions. "Fine. If you won't give her back, you'll have to deal with the consequences."

"Ha!" he scoffed. "Tìr nan Òg is losing magic, which means you don't have any to waste."

She smiled coldly. "Keeping you prisoner is never a waste, human. You have until the sun sets tomorrow to return her or I'll ensure the barrier never weakens again."

Chapter Eighteen

Who is she?

Branwen had been the first to ask the question Cäcilia should have been asking for years. Who was she? She had no idea. But she did know that she wasn't going to find answers at the back of a dark cave. She redoubled her efforts to loosen the rope. She flipped through the pictures of the knots in her mind, trying to match them to what she could feel around her wrists.

Her frustration grew as each one refused to pair. "It's like they weren't even trying to tie them properly," she muttered.

Of course. That was it. Her book had held knots that skilled sailors would know. But how many faeries were sailors? The likelihood of any of the human exiles being seamen was equally low. She tossed aside her efforts of identifying the type of knot and set to work using her understanding of knots and ropework in general to loosen her bonds.

Her lips were chapped and bleeding and her wrists rubbed raw by the time the rope fell loose to the ground. She allowed herself a few moments of resting her skin against the cool stone before tackling her ankles. With her hands now free, the second set of knots came undone much faster.

At last she was free and pushed to her feet, steadying herself against the rock wall as the blood flowed back into her legs. As much as she strained her eyes, no light filtered through to her hiding spot, and she had to fight the fear that she would be lost in the recesses of the mountain forever. She pressed her hand into the wall, absorbing the feel of the stone. Her fingers found smooth ridges and bumps, like cake batter had solidified.

The light draft she had felt earlier tickled the hairs on her arms, teasing a way out. She undid what remained of her braid, letting her hair pool on the ground around her feet. She had no way of marking her trail to keep from being lost, so her hair would have to suffice.

With one hand on the wall of the cave and her hair stretching out behind her, she probed the ground with each foot before stepping. The rock pricked her soles, but not enough to cut. Her confidence in navigating the cave grew with each step, though her trepidation in what lay ahead swelled along with it.

Her captors didn't know she couldn't see, and surely they hadn't planned on leaving her tied in the back of the cave to rot away forever. So at some point, they would be coming back. And what if a guard had been posted at the exit? How could she slip past them?

As much as she wanted to formulate a plan ahead of time, she did not have enough information to do so, and she pushed the thoughts away as her heart raced with anxiety.

And then her foot slipped off the rock into warm, running water.

She stumbled back with a small shriek that echoed up and down the tunnel.

Kneeling on the ground, she ran her hand over the wall until she found the opening that allowed the water to flow through. It was larger than she had expected, and she couldn't reach the other side of the stream with her hand. But the water wasn't deep, burbling across the path before disappearing through the opposite wall.

As she prodded around, new sounds joined the water and her pounding pulse. Voices. She leaned forward and stuck her head in the narrow opening where the water came from. The scent of rotten eggs grew stronger, though the sounds faded. Quickly she pulled back, hoping to free her nose from the noxious smell.

She crawled to the other side of the tunnel and repeated her investigation. For the first time in hours, something other than darkness met her eyes. The flickering orange light was too distant to blind her, but she choked back a sob at finally seeing color again.

Voices traveled against the current of the stream, losing all distinguishing words. The raucous tones made her shiver. She sat back on her heels.

The way out lay ahead, though most certainly blocked by at least one guard. Downstream led to fresh air and fire...and more of her captors.

Upstream offered nothing but darkness and a scent that made her eyes water.

But it also promised freedom.

She wrapped a fistful of hair around her mouth and nose to block out some of the smell and crouched down. The narrow opening was large enough for her slender frame, and the warmth of the water under her hands and knees made the experience not as unpleasant as it could have been.

The rotten egg odor was not as bad as she'd expected, and the tunnel did not close in on her as she'd feared, so she was able to follow the slight upward slope with no difficulty. She did wish she had taken the time to braid her hair again, as it was dragging through the water.

"...I don't get why we got to check on her though. She can't exactly escape without getting past us."

"Boss's orders."

The voices came out of nowhere, followed by heavy steps as the speakers crossed the stream. She ducked her head around to see the faint glow of light pass from view, reflecting off the water and something dark and rippling.

Her hair.

She wasn't far enough up the stream for all her hair to be out of sight. Slowly, with as little noise as she could manage, she pulled the long strands toward her.

Panting, she debated what to do. Should she hide in silence until they came back?

But once they reached the cave, they would know she was gone. And this stream was her only way out. Now was her only chance to put some distance between her and them.

She crawled faster, not worrying about how much noise she made for the moment. Even if they couldn't fit in the tunnel as far as she could, they might still be able to reach her hair and pull her back.

After a few minutes, shouts echoed from the main tunnel, and she plastered herself to the wall in an effort to hide from any light. The men splashed through the stream again as they hurried out of the cave.

She crawled along, her wet hair weighing her down. She closed her eyes against the stinging air, trusting her sense of place more than her vision anyway. Her hands slipped on the wet stone, and her legs and feet bore many scrapes. Soon, though, fresh air mingled with the scent of rotten eggs, and the rough ground turned to soft soil. She pulled herself upright and took a deep breath.

She'd made it! All on her own, she'd escaped!

A giggle of glee tumbled from her mouth, and she danced a few steps of joy.

But she was still trapped on the wrong island. Darkness was her greatest enemy, but it was also her ally. She needed to find a new hiding place until she could get back to Peadar.

Her hair was too wet to do much with it, but she twisted it into a quick braid as she plotted her next steps. The exiles were below her, so she determined to find a path that led up. While the stream had helped once, the water was undrinkable, so she would need to find a better source soon.

With that in mind, she turned away from the cliff she'd emerged from and stepped into the depths of the jungle. Her hair caught on a branch and she turned to loosen it, only to freeze at the sound of a stick breaking behind her.

A hand clamped over her mouth to stop her from screaming, but she couldn't have made a sound if she'd tried.

Chapter Nineteen

Peadar did his best to keep the telltale glow of his wings to a minimum as he skimmed the tops of the trees. Behind him, the Lost Boys fanned out, keeping distance between them to not draw attention as they prepared to cross the narrow strait that separated the two islands.

The barrier brushed over him with barely a hint of resistance. He growled under his breath at the failing magic. This was more than his ability to keep them contained. This was Tìr nan Òg itself failing.

And he had no idea what to do about it.

He wasn't king of the faeries or even lord of one of the greater regions. He'd lost that opportunity when he'd chosen the wrong side years ago, when he was young and foolish. If he were being honest, his punishment was more than fair — he could have had his own collar of iron for what he did.

But Cäcilia didn't deserve to be in the middle of all this. Humans in Tìr nan Òg never fared well, and he had unwittingly brought her to the worst place possible.

No, he was still a fool. He knew the barrier had weakened; he should have known the exiles would have figured that out as well and taken advantage of it. Although none of that explained how they knew she was there.

Something else was going on, if he could only figure out what.

He circled the volcano, looking for any signs of Cäcilia. Several fires burned, marking gatherings of the exiles along the beach, but he didn't dare get any closer. A soft glowing beacon caught his eye, and he veered toward it. The Lost Boy Maelore's tracking magic must have revealed something. Peadar landed softly in the small clearing, hiding his wings to limit the light the gathering faeries gave off.

Maelore pointed to the trampled bushes that led off into the jungle. A single strand of impossibly long brown hair lay over a footprint that could only have belonged to a human. A fire filled him, and he clenched his hands to stop them from shaking. Where had they taken her?

"Maelore, you follow the trail and see where it leads. The rest of us will fan out and see what else we can find near here."

The small faery nodded once and darted into the jungle, his wings a barely discernible brown glow among the foliage. Peadar knelt and picked up the strand of Cäcilia's hair. He'd never noticed any falling out before. Had it caught on something that pulled it free? Or had her captor ripped it out?

He bundled the length in his hand and paced the small open area as he fought the rising tightness in his chest. If they hurt her... He still wasn't ready to evaluate why it mattered so much, but it did. She mattered.

Something tickled his nose, and he reached up to brush it aside, only for his fingers to tangle in another piece of hair. He gathered it up, holding it tight to his chest, the need to protect every piece of her filling him.

But where had she come from? He lifted into the air, risking the light of his wings as he searched for a reason she would have been in the small clearing. He could find no trace of a trail or spot to camp. Dropping back to the ground, he probed the darkness for more signs of her, kicking himself for not noting where the hair had been. A sharp odor reached him, but he ignored it. He pushed aside branches and ducked under large leaves until he found another.

This time he didn't pull it, instead following it to see where it led.

A rock wall rose from the jungle, and the rotten smell grew worse, making his eyes sting. He rubbed them, continuing his search.

His foot splashed into a small stream, and he immediately dropped to his knees to splash his eyes. More strands of hair caught his fingers, and he used his wings to lighten the area.

The stream flowed straight into the rock wall, and the hairs in his hand disappeared with the water.

She'd escaped. And left him a trail to follow.

"Peadar!" The whisper reached him through the trees, and he hurried back to the clearing, where Maelore hopped on one foot.

"I found her!" he said in a loud whisper. "They have a camp hidden at the base of the mountain. She's tied up."

A roaring filled Peadar's ears, and he stumbled, catching himself on a hanging vine. He'd been so hopeful that she had gotten away.

"Something's going on," Maelore continued. "They were all arguing about something."

"We need to move fast," Peadar agreed.

"There's a lot more of them, though. I don't know if we can take them."

"We'll have to be sneaky. And I know just the thing," Peadar crowed, excitement filling him as a plan began to form.

He showed them the stream that fed from the rock.

"How do we know it goes where we want it to?" Jowan asked.

"Because Cäcilia came this way, so she escaped once."

They split up, Jowan going with Peadar and Maelore guiding the others down the volcano to encircle the camp. Eoinan would fly back to the Great Tree and gather reinforcements.

The tunnel was too small to spread his wings, and crawling downhill in the dark was disorienting, but Peadar comforted himself with the knowledge that Cäcilia had made it through.

When they reached the larger passage, they paused, listening for the correct route.

Jowan found where the stream continued, spying the reflection of the flames ahead.

"Are you sure I can't go this way?" he asked, pointing to the wider path.

"No, come on," Peadar said. "We know they're this way."

Another few minutes of crawling and breathing in the fumes that made his head light, and they reached the clearing. Peadar slipped out of the stream and hid behind a plant with large, umbrella-like leaves.

A faery tossed a log onto the fire, sending a shower of sparks that lit up the space. Maelore had been right — there were far more exiles than they'd realized. They lounged in groups or stood talking. Many had flaggons they drank from at frequent intervals.

Off to the side, partly hidden behind a pile of crates, Cäcilia sat on the ground, her hair pooling around her. A rope around her arm was looped over a staff held by a human of large proportions. He let out a slight sigh. She was okay.

Jowan nudged him, pointing to the sky. The faintest glow winked in and out, signaling the others were in place.

Peadar pulled out his short sword and threw his head back, ready to give the call to attack. A figure stepped between him and the fire, blocking the light.

The figure stopped, startled to see the faery there. "You!"

That voice.

No.

It'd been years since he'd last heard it, but he'd never forget the human that had led to his downfall.

"Phillip? You're behind all this?"

Chapter Twenty

An overwhelming sense of relief filled Cäcilia when she heard Peadar's voice only a few feet away. She pushed aside the urge to cry to focus on his words. Who was Phillip? And why did Peadar know him?

She struggled against the man holding her. They hadn't trusted her with ropes alone this time, worried that she might escape again. And she had every intention of doing so.

As more Lost Boys jumped out of the trees and the exiles leaped to defend themselves, Cäcilia struggled against the man holding her.

"Peadar, my old friend, what a surprise," the human Peadar had called Phillip said. "Dropping by for some refreshments, are you?"

"I'm not your friend, and you know why I'm here."

"Tut, tut, so impatient. Once upon a time you couldn't wait to spend time in my company."

Peadar's posture shifted, his silhouette dark against the backdrop of the fire. "I remember it the other way around."

"Do you now?" Phillip paced before the fire, swinging his sword. "Shall I remind your dear Lost Boys of what you did?"

"The faeries know what I did. Do your men know what you did? How you enslaved humans to harness the power to take over the throne of Tìr nan Òg? How you lured women and children through the portals?"

Cäcilia gasped. How could a human have done that to others? The exiles shifted uneasily as Peadar's words carried to the groups fighting each other.

Peadar raised his voice even more to reach the faeries battling in the sky. "How you stole the throne from the Daoine Sith in an attempt to rule over faery and human alike?"

The man holding Cäcilia loosened his hold as he listened to the argument.

"Yes," sneered Phillip, "and you helped me do it."

No! He wouldn't have!

"I know," Peadar said, stepping closer to him. "Because I was the one with the real power."

With that, he reached toward the fire, making it roar into the sky. Cäcilia closed her eyes against the sudden flare, even as hope filled her. He had grown since then.

The man holding her flung his hands over his eyes, letting go of her.

"Cäcilia, run!" Peadar shouted.

She grabbed her hair and ran toward his voice, praying she didn't stumble over something in the dark.

Then he was there, taking her hand in his. "Are you ready?" he asked.

"Always," she replied.

He lifted off the ground, taking her with him, and soon they were soaring through the air. The fog quickly enveloped them, and she tightened her hold on him.

"Who was that?" she asked.

He took so long to answer she thought he wasn't going to. "Someone I shouldn't have trusted."

She squeezed his hand, knowing he would tell her more when he was ready.

The sky began to lighten as the fog dissipated, and the clouds lit up in shades of pink and orange.

Eventually, Peadar set her down on the golden path between the rowan trees. He turned to her and took both her hands in his.

"Please tell me you're not hurt? I was so worried, I..."

"I'm fine," she said, smiling at his concern. "I was frightened at first. Then I remembered that I don't have to sit and wait for someone to tumble through my window to find my own way."

He ran his hand over her hair, brushing strands from her face. "You're amazing, you know that?"

Her cheeks flushed. He drew her closer, close enough she could see his green eyes. And then he leaned closer still. Her breath caught as she anticipated what would come next.

"I leave you alone for a few days, and this is the trouble you get up to?" a stern voice interrupted.

She jerked away from Peadar and turned toward the voice. A woman in all black stood with her arms folded, one finger tapping on the opposite arm.

"Amaran!" Cäcilia cried, running toward her.

"Cäcilia, no!" Peadar stopped her with a hand on her arm.

"What is it? That's my guardian."

"I know — but she's also Mara, Queen of Tìr nan Òg."

Chapter Twenty-One

P eadar clung to Cäcilia's hand, determined to never let her go again. Whatever she needed, he would do. Even if it meant giving up being lord of the Never Isles.

But he would not let Mara lock her away in a tower ever again.

The stately faery sighed dramatically. "Cäcilia, my dear. I do not understand why you felt the need to run away like that. Did you not trust me after I protected you for all those years?"

Cäcilia lifted her head, her hair tumbling gloriously to the ground in the early morning light. "I left to find you — but I learned that you were my captor. Why should I trust you?"

A flicker of guilt washed over Mara's face, though she hid it quickly. "Because I know who your real family is."

Cäcilia's hand tightened in his as she gave a little gasp. "Who are they?"

"I can take you to them right now, if you'd like." Her focus was on a spot at the edge of the golden path.

Peadar stepped forward. "You're not taking her anywhere."

Mara turned to glare at him. "You have caused enough trouble — or do you want to be exiled further?"

"Send him with me," Cäcilia blurted out.

"I beg your pardon?" Mara demanded.

But Peadar's heart threatened to drown him. She wanted him to go with her? To meet her family? "Cäcilia, I..."

"Please, Peadar? Come with me? I don't want to meet these strangers alone. I need you." Her gray eyes were focused on a point over his shoulder, but he couldn't deny the vulnerability within their depths.

He tugged her closer, his other hand covering her cheek. "I'll go wherever you go, my star."

"Are you two ready?" Mara asked with barely concealed disgust in her voice.

"Almost," Cäcilia said, turning to her. "I just have one question — why is my hair like this?" She lifted a handful of the dark tresses, the ends still curling in a pool at her feet.

A smile quirked the corner of Mara's mouth. "That's your pressing question?"

"Yes. You refused to tell me as a child, and I want to know this one thing before I go with you."

"Fine. Due to an ancient treaty, faeries are invited to the christening of all human babies, though it's mostly only ruling families who bother. If they so choose, the faeries can bless the baby with a gift. Over the years, it's become a status symbol for a faery to give a gift to babies of royal or noble birth. At yours, two argued over who would give you the most beautiful hair.

And as no two gifts can be exactly the same, you ended up with incredibly strong and fast-growing hair."

"That's it?"

"Yes, that's it. Now, are you ready?" She wasn't looking at them.

Peadar turned to see what had her focus. A large red dog sat by a rowan tree, his gaze locked on Mara. Anger flared through Peadar. "What is Cù dhearg doing here?"

"Carrying messages for me, like he always does," she retorted. "And he's saying we need to hurry up and get you back to the humans."

"Why?" Cäcilia asked. "Why the hurry?"

"Because they're at war over you, and returning you to your parents is the only way to stop it."

"You caused a war by taking a baby?" Horror filled him. This was worse than anything he had done, worse than Phillip trying to rule Tìr nan Òg.

"It wasn't supposed to go on this long," Mara explained, then made a cutting motion with her hand. "But enough of this. Are you both coming? If you choose to stay here, Peadar, you know your punishment."

"He's coming with me," Cäcilia said firmly. He thrilled at the way she refused to let him go.

"If you go, you can never come back," Mara warned.

Peadar looked around at the brightly colored trees, the rainbow clouds, the shimmering gold path beneath his feet. And then he looked at Cäcilia. "I won't need to come back. I'll be home."

Mara reached out to the rowan tree, and a doorway appeared in its trunk. Cù dhearg stepped through first, proving the impossibly narrow portal was capable of accepting them. Peadar followed, guiding Cäcilia along with him. Mara brought up the rear, closing the doorway behind her.

Peadar glanced back to see his home for the last time. The human world might not be as vibrant as Tìr nan Òg, but he knew, with Cäcilia, everything would be brighter every day for the rest of his life.

Chapter Twenty-Two

T he gentle sounds of the forest were replaced by the cold
echo of stone. Cäcilia kept her hand tucked into Peadar's,
unsure of her new surroundings. The ground under her feet was
as hard as the stones of her tower, but smoother.

"You there! Where did you come from?" Clanging metal and
heavy footsteps approached.

"We are here for an immediate audience with the president,"
Amaran announced.

"You can't just demand an audience," the guard retorted.

Amaran whispered something to him, and the guard called
for another to take them to the council room while he ran
ahead.

Amaran — Mara, Cäcilia reminded herself — swept after
him, bidding them to follow. Peadar tucked her hand in his
elbow.

"Are you all right?" he whispered.

She shook her head. She didn't know. Learning that she had parents was a huge shock. That they were nobles — that she was of noble birth of some type — was an even bigger shock. And she was about to meet them.

They paused, and Cäcilia could make out two more guards standing against the wall. Mara turned to her and placed a hand on her shoulder.

"My girl —"

"You may enter now." The first guard interrupted whatever Mara was going to say to her.

Four guards surrounded them, rigid in uniforms of gold and purple, and escorted them through the doors that opened in the wall. A massive room, filled with the murmurings of many people, swallowed them.

To Cäcilia's left, tiers of tables rose from the floor. To her right were glorious thrones on which sat the two people she'd most longed to meet.

Cäcilia swallowed hard as she approached. Should she curtsy? What did one do when meeting a president and his lady?

The next few minutes passed in a blur as the president spoke with Mara. Both voices rose and fell with hostility while she clung to Peadar's hand.

Until...

"Cäcilia?" Her name was spoken by the woman sitting beside the president, a tremulous note in her voice.

Then the woman descended and enveloped Cäcilia in her arms. "My daughter," she whispered.

Cäcilia hugged her back, uncertain as to how she felt. She'd wanted to know her parents, but the moment was too much. The murmurings from the crowd on the tiers resumed.

"Lady Sarah," the president's voice broke through. "As pleasant as this might be, we have pressing matters to discuss."

The woman pulled back, holding tightly to Cäcilia's hand. "Please. You'll be shown somewhere comfortable. I will come find you as soon as I can. Just please...don't leave again."

Cäcilia gave her a reassuring smile. She didn't know where she would go even if she could. A guard reappeared and escorted them out to the hall, where a servant in a plum-colored dress waited. She led them away from the council room and the massive hall and up a flight of stairs.

"Everything is very white here," Peadar observed as they walked arm in arm down the corridor.

The servant ahead gave a knowing smile over her shoulder as she paused to show them into another room.

"This is a private sitting room. Tea will be brought soon," the servant said before she vanished.

Cäcilia rubbed her arm.

"Are you all right?" Peadar asked.

"Yes...I'm just not sure I'll ever get used to being kept inside again."

He took her hand. "There's a large window. Maybe we can open it, and that will help."

She followed him to the bright section of the wall. He reached for it. A creaking sound was followed by a gust of fresh air, and she sighed.

"Come," he said with a tug on her hand.

She let him guide her forward, through the open window. "A balcony?" she gasped.

"Yes! It's quite large too — with a tall railing, so you shouldn't trip. Here." He led her to the edge, and she found the railing.

"Peadar…"

"Yes, my star?"

"Are you sure you will be happy here? It's so different from the Never Isles."

She sank against his chest as he wrapped his arms around her. "The Never Isles were an adventure. But it's time I grew up and stopped hiding. And there's nowhere I'd rather be than by your side."

She tilted her head up, desperate for a glimpse of his face. Although it was blurry, she could see the love printed there. "I love you," she whispered.

"I love you, too," he replied, his lips brushing against her own.

Then everything was forgotten in the bliss of his kiss.

If you want more fairy tales and sweet content, sign up for my newsletter!

www.RobynSarty.com/Peadar/

Acknowledgements

Thank you so much for reading *Of Song and Wonder*! I hope you enjoyed reading Cäcilia and Peadar's story even more than I enjoyed writing it. (And if you did enjoy it, it would mean the world to me if you would leave a review.)

I loved being able to revisit this world of magic and wonder, but this story would be nothing more than an idea if not for the support of so many people.

My thanks always and foremost to God and His goodness and mercy.

Thank you to Sarah Beran for not letting me give up on Cäcilia and Peadar. Your support and encouragement mean the world to me, and I'm eternally grateful for your friendship.

Thank you to Rebecca Goodwin and DaLeena Taylor for beta reading and helping me brainstorm the difficult things.

Thank you to Jackie, Angela N, and Sìne for answering all my questions about Scotland, Gaelic, and Scottish folklore. Any remaining errors I'm hiding under the guise of "artistic license."

Thank you to Nicole Schroeder for her incredible editing skills and supportive friendship.

And, as always, a huge thank you to my husband for his neverending support, love, and encouragement.

Robyn Sarty

January 2025

About the Author

Robyn Sarty is an avid fan of all things Disney, and she loves stories with happy endings, where good triumphs over evil. She tries to incorporate these elements into all of her writing, stories that feature women who refuse to back down from a challenge. She lives in rural Nova Scotia with her very own Prince Charming, where she is easily distracted by sparkly things and glitter. When she's not reading or writing, she can be found baking cakes, rearranging her library, or playing with her Bernese Mountain Dogs, Toblerone and Otto.

Sign up for a free short story, updates, and exclusive content
here:
https://robynsarty.com/ebook-giveaway/

www.robynsarty.com
https://www.facebook.com/RobynSartyAuthor
https://www.instagram.com/robynsarty/

A Gracious Hope

Can one find hope when everything familiar has been stripped away?

On the eve of her nineteenth birthday, Alora learns she's not a peasant girl, the people who raised her aren't even related to her, and she can't marry the boy from the village who promised to return for her. She's a princess, betrothed to a neighboring royal — and cursed since birth.

But Alora adores her simple life and flees from her newfound expectations. When the curse is enacted anyway, she must fight her way through a strange new land. If she doesn't defeat the one who cursed her, she'll be trapped in a dream forever.

A Gracious Hope, *a retelling of Sleeping Beauty and* The Wizard of Oz, *is a stand-alone novella, complete with such tropes as "protective hero," "he falls first," and "no damsels here."*

https://books2read.com/AGraciousHope

Keep reading for a preview!

Chapter One

"You're the hidden princess!"

Nineteen years of lies, and they decided now was the best time to tell her.

Now, the day before her nineteenth birthday, when she would have finally been able to follow her own dreams.

Her aunt's words rang in Alora's ears, an echoing chorus to remind her she'd never had a choice.

She certainly hadn't reacted like a princess, directing her outburst at her poor aunt and uncle. Although it served them right, keeping a secret like that her whole life to just spring it on her now. A twinge of guilt pricked her as she remembered Aunt Em's face. The older woman had been so sure Alora would be excited for the news, and hadn't known what to do when she had refused to leave.

That refusal had lasted until the royal carriage appeared and she'd discovered she really didn't have a choice. Not about staying with the only family she'd ever known. Not about being a royal. Not about the betrothal that was part of Em's excited announcement.

"I made you a dress for your birthday." Aunt Em had handed her a bundle of pink and blue fabric. "It's like your hydrangeas."

Hydrangeas.

Of all the things Aunt Em thought she would miss, she chose the hydrangeas.

Ever since Alora was a child, the flowers on either side of the door into their thatched cottage had grown curiously. Pink on one side, blue on the other, as though the two sides warred.

The dress she wore reflected that battle.

The material was of far greater quality than any she'd worn before, but the design was wholly the homey, heartfelt creation of her aunt.

Yesterday, Alora would have loved it. Today, it broke her heart.

The road under the carriage changed from smooth dirt to cobblestones that jarred her teeth, pulling her back to the present. A cheer went up as the procession passed. She shrank back farther into the luxurious cushions and clenched her fist, willing the burning in her eyes to dissipate. She would not let these city dwellers see her pain. At least none of the guards had insisted on riding in the carriage with them.

"Nearly there now," Aunt Em said from the opposite bench. She offered Alora a nervous smile.

"You've been here before." Why the thought surprised her, she wasn't sure, but she wished she'd thought of it before rebuffing all her aunt's attempts at conversation during the long journey.

"Of course." Now that Alora had broken her silence, Aunt Em relaxed into her usual fussy self. She reached over and smoothed the rich silk of Alora's skirt — the blue side. "But it's been nearly twenty years; I'm sure much has changed."

"Will you stay with me?" Alora asked. She adjusted the two-toned skirt so her aunt wouldn't detect the paper hidden in the pocket.

Aunt Em shook her head, sadness cloaking her careworn frame. "I have to return before nightfall. You know how your uncle worries when I'm not home."

"What will I do without you?" She hated that she sounded like a child.

"Oh, my dear." Aunt Em squeezed her hand. "You'll have your mother, someone new to guide you, and a handsome young prince. You'll do well enough without me, I'm sure."

Alora flopped back against the seat. She didn't *want* someone new. Or a prince. "How do you know he's handsome? Maybe he's old and ugly."

"He's not old; he was just a baby when you were born. But as for looks, well, you know that beauty is fleeting."

Alora scrunched her nose. Aunt Em had started saying that long ago, when people first began noticing Alora's looks. At first it was just adults commenting on how pretty she was as a child. But as she grew, the boys started paying her more and more attention whenever she went to the little village. The village where she first met —

The skrill of bagpipes interrupted her thoughts. The carriage made a sharp turn, and a shadow passed over the windows. She peered out, eager for a distraction from her thoughts. They'd gone under the massive archway leading to the castle. Rows of smartly dressed pipers in their kilts and jackets lined the road, and bugle calls heralded them as they drew closer to the castle.

Ahead, a stone structure loomed. Craning her head, Alora peered up at the many towers that rose from the rooftops, silhouetted against the cloudy sky. Each was decked with bunting, and silk flags snapped in the breeze. Despite the overcast day, sunlight glinted off the multitudes of polished windows, forcing her to look away. But no matter where she looked, all she saw was more evidence of opulence and riches, from the pristine gardens to the gleaming marble staircase.

She pushed away from the window, suppressing a shudder. She didn't belong in this world. Aunt Em looked ready to speak, but there wasn't time. The carriage lurched to a stop amid a crescendo from the bagpipes. Then the door opened, and someone announced "Her Royal Highness, Alora Gwenyth Liana Canmore, the Princess of Dunkeld" for all to hear.

Alora stared at her aunt in horror. Was *that* how she would be called from now on?

Chapter Two

Alora froze in the carriage door, unable to move. This couldn't be happening. No. She wasn't that person with the ridiculous title. She was just Alora, plain and simple. Her chest constricted, and she couldn't breathe.

"Out! Out!" Aunt Em hissed, pushing her toward the door.

A white glove appeared as she clambered for something to hold onto. She took the proffered hand and stepped out, missing the narrow step and landing heavily on the ground. She staggered forward until a second hand caught her about the waist.

The instant she was steady, the hand vanished. Alora turned to offer her thanks, but the stern-faced guard at her side didn't even glance at her. She released his other hand and stepped forward, finally taking in the scene before her.

Large sweeping stairs rose to the front of the castle. The people gathered on the terrace were both more and fewer than she'd thought. She had hoped for a quiet chance to meet with the king and queen to discuss the error they'd made; she'd feared throngs of people would be there to gawk at her arrival.

Instead, about twenty people stood at various levels on the stairs to greet her. At the top were the king and queen. Alora ignored the rest as she climbed the steps, ready to give the royal couple a piece of her mind.

The dainty shoes Aunt Em had insisted she wear forced her to make her ascent slower than she would have liked, and she felt as though the entire kingdom stared at her. Whispers from the nobles who stood on the steps reached her.

"Raised as a peasant, poor girl."

"At least she's pretty."

"That *dress*."

Her spine bristled at that comment. Say what they liked about her, but how dare they mock Aunt Em's hard work. Even if it was a bit...unusual.

At last she reached the top of the stairs. Before she could say anything, the queen wrapped her arms about Alora in a weepy hug.

"Oh my dear girl, *how* I have missed you."

Alora froze. Missed her? This woman didn't even *know* her!

At last the queen pulled back. Tears filled her eyes as she regarded Alora, one hand on her mouth, the other cupping Alora's shoulder. Alora stared back in surprise. She *did* know this woman. Just not as the queen.

Many years ago, when Alora was still young enough to attend the village school, a woman had visited on occasion, bringing books for the schoolhouse. She had never said who she was, but the children had delighted in coming up with all sorts of tragic backstories for the kind but enigmatic stranger. The most popular ones labeled her as a widow who'd lost her child.

Well, they'd been partly right.

"My dear Alora." The deep voice broke through the awkward reunion. The king offered her his hand. She took it and curtsied as she'd been taught.

"None of that, child. You're family," he said, drawing her up.

At least he didn't try to hug her.

"Let us introduce you to a few of our key members of court." With a hand on her back, the king turned her to face the first of the nobles approaching. The lord of something or other pressed both her hands between both of his as he bowed in greeting. The movement was repeated by each of the nobles she was introduced to.

What followed was a whirlwind of names and faces, none of which she remembered. She was more interested in sneaking glances at the king and queen, seeking some confirmation they were her true parents.

The king's graying hair held hints of blond like her own, and her blue eyes matched the queen's. But heaps of people had blond hair or blue eyes. It was far from proof.

Still, no one else questioned her right to be there.

It didn't matter. Daughter of the king and queen or no, she didn't *want* to be there. Surely her wishes would be considered at some point.

Wouldn't they?

"Alora, allow me to introduce you to Laelynn. She'll be your companion for the next few days until you're settled."

Alora looked up to see a young woman only a few years her senior. She was exquisitely beautiful with rich, dark curls, and warm brown eyes. She curtsied, but her eyes remained locked on Alora's as she suppressed a smile. "Your Highness."

"P-pleased to meet you." Alora curtsied in return, ducking her head to hide the pink that flamed her cheeks. Her speech troubles had faded as she grew, but being on display had brought them back. Thankfully few people had expected her to say much thus far.

The introductions had slowly been leading her closer to the grand doors, and she cast about in search of Aunt Em. She had hopes of sneaking back with her, but at least she wanted to say goodbye.

"Come, you must be tired from the drive," Laelynn said. "There's time for a rest, then you can change out of this...dress." Her tone was kind, but her eyes flicked over the dress dismissively.

Alora clutched the skirts. "Aunt Em made it for me."

"Yes, of course. It's...lovely." Laelynn's own dress was a soft pink, the style simple and elegant. None of the ruffles and bows that adorned Alora's own. Yet it also seemed fancier than the event required, perhaps due to the slight shimmer in the material.

Laelynn tucked Alora's arm under her own and pulled her inside the castle. The nobles followed a few steps behind.

The entrance hall was nearly the full height of the castle, with tall, narrow windows that filled the room with light. Between every window was a golden brazier that held a lit torch despite the hour. The flames reflected off the white stone, filling the room with a warm glow.

Servants lined the walls, bowing and curtsying as they walked. Even they were dressed in nicer clothing than anything Alora had worn at home, but mostly she envied their sensible shoes. She tried not to limp as the ridiculous things she wore pinched her toes and rubbed her heels.

The door slammed shut behind them, and she turned around. "Where's Aunt Em?"

Laelynn patted her arm. "I'm sure she'll be along shortly. The king will want to speak to her about your journey."

"Why?"

"Nothing to worry about," Laelynn reassured her.

No? Then why were there so many guards around? And why did everyone relax once the doors were shut?

Laelynn guided her up a sweeping staircase. Only a single pair of guards followed them, and Alora was grateful for the sudden silence as they walked down a carpeted hallway. The lower half of the wall was dark wood paneling, while the top half was a mural that stretched the length of the hall. It told a story, she was certain; if only she recognized it.

"Now, your birthday celebration is tomorrow, but tonight is the Presentation."

"Presentation?" Alora asked, her eyes still glued to the painting.

"Yes, of course. On the eve of their nineteenth birthday, the future monarch is presented to the people at sundown, starting a week of festivities and ceremonies." Laelynn's voice was full of excitement. Alora's stomach dropped further.

If they'd planned an entire week of celebration for her, it was going to be even harder for her to weasel out of being princess.

Keep reading
https://books2read.com/AGraciousHope

www.ingramcontent.com/pod-product-compliance
Lightning Source LLC
Chambersburg PA
CBHW052010240626
47153CB00008B/2815